Praise for Marie Tre

"An old-fashioned gothic rom.... with a time-travel twist, GOTHIC DRAGON is simply fun...Marie Treanor has written a witty and sensuous tale!"

~ *Courtney Michelle, Romance Reviews Today*

Rating: 83 "The premise is most interesting indeed and Ms Treanor manages to keep things interesting right to the last page. The set-up and the way the story twists and turns are what makes Gothic Dragon a very interesting read.... I certainly find the very nature of the story interesting enough and the execution of the story entertaining enough to remember the author's name."

~ *Mrs. Giggles*

"A thrilling, sexy tale... Drago is incredibly sexy... The sex is steamy and thrilling. If you have ever wondered what would happen after a book ends this is the story that will tell you. It is a very well written piece that will keep you turning page after page."

~ *Amy Parker, Paranormal Romance Reviews*

Look for these titles by *Marie Treanor*

Now Available:

Killing Joe

Ariadne's Thread

The Devil and Via

Queen's Gambit

Coming Soon:

Requiem for Rab

Gothic Dragon

Marie Treanor

A Samhain Publishing, Ltd. publication.

Samhain Publishing, Ltd.
577 Mulberry Street, Suite 1520
Macon, GA 31201
www.samhainpublishing.com

Gothic Dragon
Copyright © 2009 by Marie Treanor
Print ISBN: 978-1-60504-283-1
Digital ISBN: 978-1-60504-076-9

Editing by Linda Ingmanson
Cover by Anne Cain

First Samhain Publishing, Ltd. electronic publication: July 2008
First Samhain Publishing, Ltd. print publication: May 2009

Dedication

To my husband, as always

Chapter One

The world swayed and swung back into clarity with a silent jolt, perfectly timed with the lurch of Esther's stomach.

The book on the shining mahogany table had vanished. Instead of reading, Esther stared in astonishment at the most beautiful male she had ever seen—a boy on the cusp of manhood. Dramatic black curls tumbled around his pale, tear-stained face. A high forehead swept down to perfectly arched black eyebrows and large liquid brown eyes widening with a shock that didn't quite overlay the terrible sorrow. He had bone structure to die for. A straight thin nose divided his face with a hint of arrogance. His frozen lips were full with the promise of sensuality. A young but huge personality that couldn't, and wouldn't, be ignored. Youth distracted from some deep, wild grief that could break even a stranger's heart...

Involuntarily, Esther's lips fell apart. The boy's gaze flickered to them, breaking his shock, opening the way for shame and anger. And the anger was scary, contorting his mouth, blazing out of his eyes with all the force of a volcano.

He lunged forward. For the first time, Esther registered their surroundings: darkness, save for two flaring candles that cast a pale, flickering glow across his face. As he leapt toward her from the large, raised bed, his loose, white shirt gaped open at the chest and she saw that the boy already had a man's strength.

In panic, she stumbled backward. Again the world swayed and swung. She heard her own gasp as she found herself staring at the printed page of the book she'd just dropped on the table.

The darkness, the beautiful boy, had vanished like a switched-off screen.

She must have fallen asleep for an instant...but what a strange, vivid dream!

"Miss Conway?"

Lady Hay's sudden call made Esther jump, dragged her out of the last clinging fingers of the dream. How often had her hostess spoken already? She was walking across the library from the doorway, a social smile on her face.

"Did you find what you were looking for?"

Esther pulled herself together. After all, she'd struck gold here—God knew how she'd managed to fall asleep!—and she wasn't about to let the opportunity slip.

"Wow, yes, I did," she exclaimed. "You've got a positive treasure-trove of stuff here. Not just concerning Margaret Marsden, of course."

"I know. My husband has always been an inveterate collector." Lady Hay cast a telling, not altogether affectionate glance around the book shelves which lined all four walls from plush-carpeted floor to great high ceiling.

Esther's heart twinged with more than a hint of envy. To have a library like this in your own home was a privilege she could never hope to share. Hastily, she waved her hand at the book she'd just dropped.

"This alone is a wonderful discovery. I didn't know there were any copies left of *The Prince of Costanzo*. I've been hunting all over, from the British Library down."

Lady Hay frowned slightly with the apparent effort of remembering something she wasn't terribly interested in. She picked up the book, closed it and examined the cover. "Yes, I believe it came from another collector, along with some Marsden private papers. That was my husband's Gothic literature phase. He'll be very interested to hear about your book. You said you're actually a descendent of Margaret Marsden? Is that what drew you to write about her?"

"I suppose it is, yes. But I doubt your husband will be interested in a modern work of Gothic fiction. I'm researching for a novel based on her life, not a biography."

"Forgive me, I get my Margaret Marsdens all mixed up with my Anne Radcliffes and Clara Reeves. Is she the one who got depressed and disappeared?"

"That's right. After her husband forbade her to write any more. I thought it would be fun to find a fictional solution to the mystery of her disappearance."

Lady Hay looked somewhat dubiously at all the papers and books on the big, mahogany desk. "Couldn't you just make something up, without all this...?"

"I want to make it believable." With a quick glance at her watch, Esther added, "But I see it's after five now. I won't keep you. Would it be all right to come back in the morning? I would really like to take a couple of days to study these."

"Of course," said Lady Hay graciously. "Come back tomorrow at nine, if you like. If I'm not around, my housekeeper will be. Just leave these on the table—they'll be waiting for you tomorrow."

"Thanks, you're very kind!" With a quick smile, Esther grabbed her jacket and bag and followed Lady Hay out of the library. At the door, she turned, unable to resist a last glance at the rare book she'd managed to fall asleep over—Margaret Marsden's missing novel.

It looked so ordinary in its faded cloth binding, that she could understand her hostess's lack of appreciation.

In the large hall, Lady Hay offered her hand with another social smile and a gracious "Good-bye."

Esther took the slightly limp fingers, murmuring her own farewell.

"That's an interesting ring," Lady Hay observed unexpectedly, gazing at Esther's hand as she slid it free.

"Family heirloom," Esther said. "In fact, my mother claims it belonged to Margaret Marsden."

"Really?" Frowning, Lady Hay continued to stare at it, making Esther self-conscious. She wished she'd filed her nails. "But she was early nineteenth century, wasn't she? This looks far older."

"Fifteenth century," Esther agreed. Reluctantly, she lifted her hand to display the ring. It was a vivid blue, oval-shaped lapis lazuli in a carved gold setting, large enough to be eye-catching without appearing vulgar. Close-up, the gold work was intricate and beautiful, the central stone casting a darker blue shadow that reflected her eyes.

Esther brought up her other hand and released the ring's catch. The stone swung back revealing a tiny chamber inside.

"It's a poison ring," she explained. "I can see why it would have appealed to Margaret."

"Hmm...valuable, too. Italian... You should be careful."

"I know." She wasn't even sure why she'd worn it today. Normally, she saved it for weddings and special events, but when she'd been getting ready to come here, to what was the best collection of material relating to Margaret Marsden, she'd felt she needed a good luck charm.

It had worked, too. With only a phone call to follow up her original unanswered letter, Sir Ian Hay's wife had let her into their library right away and shown her their treasures, which turned out to be greater even than she'd hoped for.

She just knew this novel was going to be special, better than anything she'd ever written.

ω

She found Kevin in the village pub, imaginatively named Ye Olde Inn, where they'd rented a room for a couple of nights. In the midst of a tea-time rush of at least twelve people, he was sitting in morose isolation at a table near the window, staring into his barely-touched pint glass.

Inexplicably, her spurt of euphoria faded. There would be no pleasure in her discovery if Kevin was still miserable about being here...

"There you are," he said with relief, standing as soon as he saw her. "Let's go upstairs and change."

"Could do," she agreed, "but I'd quite like a drink first—just one while you finish your pint. It's all right," she added as he began fishing patiently in his pocket. "I'll get it."

A moment later, she sat down beside him with her gin and lime. "Cheers!"

He gave a small smile. "You seem pleased with yourself. I take it you found something in the library? I passed it by the way—couldn't find you there."

Esther blinked. "Couldn't find me where?"

"In the public library."

It was silly to be hurt. He'd never been interested in her writing and rarely listened to anything to do with it. It had been a major breakthrough to get him down here at all. He'd only come because it was on the way to his friend's wedding at the weekend.

In a habitual nervous gesture, she began to unpin and re-pin her thick, blonde hair more securely behind her head. "I wasn't *at* the public library," she answered with careful mildness. "I was in a private library in the home of a collector. Sir Ian Hay, the oil man."

Kevin paused with his lips still on the glass, then slowly lowered it, staring at her. "You didn't tell me that."

"Yes, I did," Esther said patiently. "It's the reason I wanted to come here. Hay's made a unique collection of Gothic literature, and he's got the best stuff on Margaret Marsden. He's got private letters relating to her work, letters to publishers, a journal, a 'lost' book, story plans—"

"Did you meet him?" Kevin interrupted.

"Who? Hay? No, he's away. It was his wife who—"

"I wish you'd told me before. I could have gone there with you."

"To look at a bunch of mouldering papers and old books? Not your usual style, Kevin."

"I'd like to have seen the house, though," he muttered, burying his face back in his pint.

He'd have liked to meet people of wealth and title, an oil industry giant like Sir Ian Hay. It was an irritating trait, especially combined with his disinterest in her work.

Why am I marrying this guy?

You're not. You're engaged to him and have been for more than two years.

Impulsively, she opened her mouth to ask the questions that had been nagging her consciously and unconsciously for so long. *When are we going to get married? Kevin, do you want to marry me?*

But at the last minute she shied away. She didn't really want to know the answers.

What came out instead was, "You can drive me out there tomorrow morning, if you like. You'd see the house then."

He blinked at her. "You're going back?"

"Kevin, I was only there for half an hour. Not nearly long enough to actually study the stuff. I need to go back tomorrow and probably the day after, too."

"We're due at Steve's on Friday," he said frostily.

"Well, it's only Wednesday today. We can easily get to Steve's on Friday evening, and the wedding's not till Saturday at four."

"And what do you suggest *I* do while you bury yourself in all this nonsense?"

She'd told him her plan when she'd booked the room here. But he hadn't been listening. He'd intended staying one night and moving on to Steve's tomorrow for more civilized entertainment.

Stupidly, she'd thought this might have been a romantic break. Stupidly, she'd imagined he got that.

"It's a nice place, Kevin," she said lightly. "Relax, go for walks, read, all the things you've got no time for in the city. And you can drop me off and pick me up at the Hall—you might get to meet the Hays that way."

He glanced at her, clearly resentful, suspicious and just a little hopeful. Honesty compelled her to add, "Though I'll just be going straight to the library, you know, not entertained to tea."

15

He drew in a breath. "Esther, don't you think this stuff's gone far enough? Why don't you concentrate on your real work and give up the writing nonsense?"

"I have had a little success already," she said.

He snorted. "E-books. Who's ever heard of e-books? How can you show these off on your coffee-table? Esther, you have a chance of *running* Nailand & Burke—in time—with just a little effort. Don't waste your talents on this other stuff. It's time to face facts: I know you're good, but you're never going to make it as a writer."

ω

Yesterday's delight in her find was notably absent as she sat in Hay's library the following morning. Although it hadn't amounted to a fight—it never did because she always backed down—last night's discussion with Kevin had left a bitter taste in her mouth. Stubbornness had brought her back here in the glare of Kevin's sulk, but all the self-doubts which had been in abeyance while she lost herself in Margaret's story resurfaced and haunted her—fully backed by the knowledge that even her fiancé had no faith in her.

Time to call it a day, Esther. Face the real world.

She felt a little like Margaret Marsden herself, forbidden to write by her husband.

With a twisted smile, she picked up an envelope at random. Extracting the paper from its acid-free protection, she discovered it to be a letter from a physician to Margaret's husband, Lord Hawton. A quick glance at the date showed her it was written during Margaret's depression, not long before her disappearance.

Interest twinged. A word caught her eye and she was lost.

Time and place disappeared for her as, with rising excitement, she followed the trail of hints and clues and definite description. When someone actually came into the library, it took her a moment to remember where she was, and who her visitor was likely to be.

A tall, distinguished man walked toward her—grey at the temples, prosperous and spreading slightly in his middle years, a frown of controlled displeasure on his cold face. Esther sprang to her feet.

"My name is Ian Hay," said her visitor abruptly.

"Hello. I'm Esther Conway—and I really appreciate being allowed into your library. This is fascinating stuff."

Deeply involved as she was, she spoke from the heart. Hay's frown twitched, and for a second Esther thought she'd sounded too enthusiastic and made herself ridiculous. Any fool could see he wasn't exactly pleased to find her there. Lady Hay had made a mistake—possibly deliberately—in letting her in.

"My wife tells me you're writing a book."

"About Margaret Marsden, yes." She felt her hands rise nervously to re-secure her hair and had to make a conscious effort to lay them back in her lap.

"We don't normally allow visitors. Not without personal introductions."

"I know, Lady Hay explained that. It was just I had the chance to come over in this direction and a friend—Professor MacGowan, she's an old colleague of my parents—mentioned your collection. I wrote, and then phoned when I arrived in the village..."

"I've been away," Hay said brusquely. Now he thought she'd taken advantage of his absence to get round his wife...

She swallowed. "I understand your concerns. I've no idea of the monetary value of such collections as yours, but in any other terms they're priceless."

For some reason, this seemed to mollify him, as if it proved her to be harmless.

Coming farther into the room, he said, "My wife was swayed beyond our normal customs by the fact that you're some sort of descendent of Margaret Marsden."

"Yes, my mother traced the family tree back that far."

"Then you are in fact related to the earls of Hawton?"

Esther laughed. "I suppose I must be, very distantly, but we don't acknowledge each other."

A faint smile curved Hay's lips. His gaze slid down to the table, as though checking on her care of the valuable documents she was rifling.

"Anything of particular interest to you?" he enquired.

"Oh yes! Some of these disagree with the accepted view of Margaret's illness after she was forbidden to write. Her doctor seems to be treating something like catalepsy. I'm just wondering if her 'decline' was a story given out by the family—to cover for her absence when she disappeared altogether."

Hay inclined his head. Reaching down, he idly picked up the "lost" book, *The Prince of Costanzo*. "And where do you think she disappeared *to*?"

Esther took a deep breath. "I'm beginning to think she didn't disappear at all. That she finally died and was buried quietly, with the whole thing hushed up by the family who'd been pretending for months—if not years—that she wasn't there."

Hay actually smiled. "You know, I wondered about that myself. I've come across no proof, though." He opened the book in his hands. "Have you had a chance to read this?"

"Not yet, but I'm *so* delighted to have found it. I didn't know it was extant anywhere."

"Nor does anyone else. That's its security. It's the only one in existence and it is truly priceless. I know of several collectors who would pay extraordinary sums to receive it, no questions asked. So I don't normally show it, even to those with introductions."

"Well, you'll have to search me when I leave," Esther said lightly. Unexpectedly, Hay smiled.

"Oh I don't think that will be necessary. Actually, it's a pleasure to meet a fellow enthusiast. In fact, if you're free tonight, my wife and I are having a few people 'round for drinks—if you'd care to join us."

Esther closed her mouth before her jaw fell all the way to the floor. "Thank you," she said faintly. "You're very kind. But since I'll have deserted him all day, I'd better keep my fiancé company..."

"Bring him," said Hay, closing the book and laying it back down in front of her. "Around seven. Dress doesn't have to be formal. Pleasure to meet you, Miss Conway."

Esther stared after his retreating back in some awe. Looked like Kevin would forgive her after all.

Slowly, she dropped her gaze to the book in front of her. Her ideas for the novel were changing in light of what she'd discovered this morning. Almost idly, she picked up *The Prince of Costanzo*. She'd wanted to read it for years and yet yesterday, when she'd finally had it in her grasp, she'd fallen asleep at Chapter One. And dreamed of that haunting young man. He had been so vivid, so real. She could remember every tragic line on his tear-streaked face, the angry twist of his lips, the intensity of his wild, dark eyes. How could her imagination have conjured up so much detail? It wasn't as if she'd ever encountered anyone remotely like him in real life...

With the spine supported in her palm, Esther let the book fall open. She knew the story, of course, having read about it in various contemporary journals. A Gothic tale set in an Italian Renaissance principality. Young English heroine, Matilda, is taken there by her widowed mother with whom Prince Rudolfo had fallen in love. But shortly after the wedding, Rudolfo is poisoned by his own illegitimate son, Drago, a young but immensely sinister individual of brutal habits and dark, supernatural tendencies. Drago then tyrannizes over the principality as well as over Matilda and her mother, until by magical means he kills off the older lady, too. Fortunately there is Rudolfo's nephew, Cosimo, who, supported by his upright English tutor John Fortune, eventually defeats Drago and frees Matilda. Matilda then marries her true love, John Fortune and returns to England with him.

The print danced before Esther's eyes. Dark and clear against the fine quality white paper, it had hardly faded at all in the two hundred years of its life. Esther wondered if she had time to read the book from the beginning and still be able to go through the rest of the documents...

Lifting her right hand, she touched the paper. A glimmer of sunlight peeked through the imperfectly closed vertical blinds on the tall windows behind her and winked on the gold of her ring, shooting a shaft of pale blue across the page. Esther began to turn the pages back to the beginning, but her hand faltered, felt suddenly heavy. She didn't seem able to move it.

The world spun around her, weighing her down. She fought it, believing she was about to faint, but nothing could stop the spinning, only time...

She landed with a jolt on something hard. The sharpness of

a stone jabbed into the palm of her hand. Noise filled her ears; heat consumed her body.

"Get out of the way, girl," someone shouted, and glancing up against the glaring sun, she saw the anxious, wrinkled face of a man. Deeply browned by the sun, he wore a thin, dirty cloth cap and some sort of smock. "They're coming."

"Who's coming?" Esther asked vaguely. She seemed to have fallen onto hard, warm earth. *In the Hays' library?*

"The prince, of course. And he'll ride you down as soon as look at you, so get yourself off the road!"

Even as she began to pull herself up, the man grabbed at her arm, dragging her back. Instinctively, Esther resisted, but the sudden sound of galloping hooves—many galloping hooves—bearing down on them, sent her scuttling to the side of the road with her anxious saviour.

What the hell's going on? Am I dreaming again?

It was too strange for fear, and there wasn't any time. She realized several people were scuttling away from the road, a swish of long skirts, a patter of bare feet disappearing into various hovels that lined the mud track. Doors slammed, frightened faces lurked behind tiny windows.

Behind the houses rose majestic green hills, beautiful and spectacular under the relentless brightness of the sun. It was hot, too hot for England. Far too hot for Scotland.

The thundering of the horses' hooves was deafening, vibrating the ground under her feet. The old man continued to tug at her arm. "Come on, come on!"

"No, wait, I want to see..." Since she was dreaming, she didn't feel compelled to share the old man's fears. Instead, she wanted to see what her mind would conjure up to have sent all these scared people scuttling for cover.

21

And then she'd wake up because she had a book to read.

The horsemen erupted round the corner, and the old man abandoned her, scurrying into the house behind them and slamming the door hard.

It was a troop of armoured soldiers, like some medieval re-enactment group, a banner of a black dragon on a red background blazing from their midst. Only the horseman in the lead wore no helmet, or indeed head covering of any kind. Thick black hair streamed out behind him. Though the pace was furious, he rode at ease, holding the reins in one hand while the other rested on his leather-clad thigh, his movements at one with the horse's rhythm.

Suddenly he didn't seem like a dream. He looked very real and solid. They all did, sun glinting off breast plates and assorted weapons, carrying with them all the force and brutality of medieval soldiery.

Esther's hand crept to her throat. The leader's head moved from one side to the other, as though quartering the village, till his restless gaze fell on her like a blow. He shouted out and her heart lurched, drumming so furiously that it almost drowned out the sounds of hooves and snorting as the troop came to a furious halt in the road right beside her.

The leader, now several yards in front of her, turned his horse and stared directly at Esther. Her stomach twisted, but she forced herself to glare back.

He was not a comfortable sight. His very poise seemed to ooze some hidden threat. And despite his stillness, raw energy, barely-controlled excitement, radiated from him with a power that was palpable.

Weapons hung at either side of his belt. His long, curling black hair fell in tangles around his shoulders. He looked young and arrogant and devastatingly handsome, although a short, black beard hid part of his strong jaw and chin. Esther found it hard to breathe, for surely it was triumph which glared at her out of his wild, blazing eyes.

"Bring her to me."

It was terse, peremptory, overlaid with the same triumph, and his gaze never left her as he gave the order. The voice itself was low, deep and curiously beautiful, but she had no time to dwell on that. For with a movement so sudden it was shocking, he turned his horse, urged it forward into an immediate gallop. At the same time, two horsemen detached themselves from the troop following him and began to move toward her.

Esther stepped back involuntarily. Free of that mesmerizing stare, the full meaning of his command suddenly became clear.

Okay, she thought nervously, as they advanced upon her. *Now I'm frightened.*

She bolted.

There weren't many places to go, and not much to help a girl on foot to escape two men on horseback, but she did her best, running instinctively for the cover of the wood beyond the houses, while behind her, the drumming of the hooves grew louder and the skin prickled on the back of her neck, as though the horses were already snorting over her shoulder.

Diving into the trees, she twisted around and ran slap into another body. At the same time, a cry rent the air, then another, and as she spun around, she saw two horses running riderless through the trees.

Terrified, she thumped her hands into the chest of her captor. He made a sound like, "Ouff!" But his grasp didn't loosen. If anything it tightened as he gasped out, "I'm not going to hurt you, for God's sake! I've just saved your neck!"

Esther looked wildly around. A few men moved into the

little clearing with her and her captor, but they kept their distance. One wiped a dagger on his sleeve. They all looked as if they came from the same re-enactment group as the men who'd been chasing her.

Straining to break free of the dream, Esther shook her head and blinked several times. When nothing changed, she took a deep, shuddering breath and forced herself to relax.

"Saved me from whom?" she asked hoarsely.

Her saviour gave a lop-sided smile. "From Prince Drago, of course."

Chapter Two

Prince Drago. The wicked sorcerer-villain from *The Prince of Costanzo.*

So I'm dreaming of the book... I don't need to be afraid. I'll wake up soon...

Sensing her capitulation, her captor released her and she stepped back to examine him. A clean-shaven young man in a black tunic under a short black cloak, a sword and dagger at his belt, his face handsome—vaguely reminiscent, in fact, of the youth she had see in that first dream... But older now, without any trace of the uncontrolled grief and fury she had witnessed. Imagined. Whatever.

"And you are...?" She had to say something. A dream without participation just didn't pass the time fast enough. *Wake up! You have to tell Kevin about drinks with the Hays tonight.*

The man bowed to her elegantly. "Cosimo, nephew of the late Prince Rudolfo, at your service, my lady. How have you come to such a pass? And how can I aid you?"

"Such a pass as what?" she asked. Cosimo glanced apologetically at her body, scanning from neck to toe.

"Forgive me. I can tell by your speech that you are a lady of birth, and yet your clothing is such that I can only imagine what troubles have beset you."

Esther laughed. She rather liked this skirt—it was new and swirly and bright. And expensive. "You wouldn't believe me if I told you."

"I might."

"Maybe later." *If I haven't woken up...*

"Very well. What did you do to offend my cousin Drago?"

Esther shrugged. "Nothing. I was just there. Everyone else had the sense to clear off. They seemed petrified of him."

"With cause," Cosimo said grimly. "He's been terrorizing them for years."

"Years?" She frowned. As far as she could recall, the action of the novel had taken place over one year, from Matilda's arrival in Costanzo until her departure with John Fortune, leaving Cosimo in control of the country. "For how long has Drago been prince?"

"For seven bitter years."

"Seven! Then you never defeated him in that first year?"

"To my eternal shame and distress, no. He drove me into exile then—I barely escaped with my life. If it had not been for my tutor I would certainly have died. But I am the rightful prince and I could not leave my people to suffer under that monster—and so I have returned. For the last two years I have been trying to dislodge him, but he is powerful."

"In what way?" she asked, bewildered. Her dream was deviating from the book, as a dream surely would, but it made it harder to understand what was going on. "The people appear to detest him and you have your own forces."

Cosimo shrugged. "You are right. They do detest him, but he has used sorcery to bind the people to him. Here, this far from his centre of power, they know to keep out of his way, but closer to the castle, they cannot break free. Some spell binds them to him, and they defend themselves so vigorously from my efforts to help that I cannot break in to bring him down." He sighed. "We are making progress, but it is slow."

Glancing around at the restive men, he straightened. "Forgive my haste, madonna, but it is dangerous to linger here. We need to return to our camp. Will you trust yourself to my care?"

She was dreaming. It seemed ridiculous to point out that she didn't know him from Adam and that she refused to go anywhere with a total stranger. However, something of her confusion must have shown on her face, for he added more gently, "You are a stranger here and appear to have no protection. I do not yet know your story, but it seems to me you may be related to the lady Matilda."

It seemed as good a tale as any other. Esther nodded. "Is Matilda with you?"

"Yes." He hesitated, then, "That is, she will return to us shortly. She is currently away on a mission for our cause. Will you come?"

What the hell. With any luck I'll wake up before we get there. Or maybe it would be fun to hang in here till I meet the heroine herself.

ω

It was a long walk, for Cosimo's men had left their horses behind for reasons of stealth.

"He hears them," one of the men explained with a quick glance over his shoulder. "Even from miles away."

"Then doesn't he hear you, too?" Esther asked. "Especially when you talk?"

The man crossed himself with such a look of fear that Esther was sorry she'd teased him. It was *her* dream; she should be able to say and do what she liked. But the emotion of her dream characters looked so real that in spite of herself she felt ashamed.

Like that other dream of the youth whose imagined emotion had moved her in reality. Some dreadful furious sorrow, mingled with anger at her uninvited presence. A fierce, young man's shame at being discovered in such a state of vulnerability.

Which brought her up short. If that boy had been Cosimo, brought low by his uncle's death, or by Drago's treachery, would he recognize her?

"Have we ever met before?" she asked him abruptly.

Cosimo smiled. He had a gentle smile. In fact, in sharp contrast to his cousin's, his whole face was soothingly gentle. "No. I would have remembered."

Which meant he'd either blanked it from his mind, or she'd got it wrong. And why the hell was she even thinking about it? Just to pass the time till she got out of this wretched dream...

For much of the day, they walked through wood, which was a relief since the trees provided some shelter from the relentless glare of the sun. But it was not an easy hike. There were hills to climb, streams to ford, rough ground for a girl wearing flimsy sandals.

As they "marched" Cosimo explained that Drago had just led a raid on his main stronghold. He and his followers had been forced to escape by stealth, and while his lieutenants set up temporary camp, Cosimo attempted a counter raid on Drago's forces, now heading back to his own base at Costanzo Castle.

"But we couldn't get near him," Cosimo complained. "He

moves too fast, and he always hears me coming."

Since the soldier had said something similar, Esther frowned at him. "How?"

Cosimo shrugged. "Sorcery. He has formed some sort of magical connection with me—we were largely brought up together, you know—and he can use it to trace me almost anywhere. If I move fast, I can catch him by surprise sometimes, but today we had no luck."

By the time they reached Cosimo's temporary camp, dusk was falling. The camp was guarded by armed men who, in strange accents, asked for passwords before allowing the travellers to go on. Watchful, if more exhausted than she could ever remember of a dream, Esther noted the respect with which they treated Cosimo.

The camp itself was a tumble-down farmhouse, very like the hovels she'd seen in the village, but surrounded by tents of varying size. From one of these emerged a tall, fair man in a plain dark velvet tunic—where did her brain get its knowledge, or imagination—of fifteenth century costume? Without greeting, he barked peremptorily, "Did you get near him? Cause any damage?"

"No, he sensed us. Even at speed he had some sort of protection around them. We tried loosing an arrow, but it bounced off the air."

"Nonsense. That was taken care of. You were simply out of range."

"On the contrary," Cosimo said tiredly. "I'll tell you about it later. In the mean time, I'd like to introduce you to my discovery of the day, the lady Esther."

He stood to one side, allowing Esther a better view of the tall man who seemed to notice her for the first time. "Drago tried to capture her."

The tall man's eyebrows flew upward. "Did he, by God? And who is the lady Esther?" He came toward her as he spoke, holding out one commanding hand. Weirdly, Esther felt both attraction and repulsion, an inclination to obey by giving him her hand, a revulsion against the strange power she sensed from him. Standing frozen in her indecision, she met his piercing gaze and felt her breath catch. Something about his cold blue eyes seemed older than man.

But hey, it was a dream. He couldn't hurt her. One push and she'd wake up. It might even be worth encouraging him to do it.

Drawing in a sharp breath, Esther laid her hand in his. His skin was cold, making her shiver. He lifted her hand to his lips, then paused. After a distinct moment, he lowered it again untouched. His eyes were on the poison ring.

"Where did you get that?" he enquired evenly.

"She's related to Matilda," Cosimo interrupted.

"Ah, are you indeed?"

"Oh yes," said Esther, since she'd already said it once. *It's a dream, only a dream...*

"May I keep it for you? This camp is necessarily full of rogues..."

"No thank you," Esther interrupted, snatching her hand back. She wasn't sure why. Except that even in a dream, she wasn't going to give up her ring to anyone.

"This is my most trusted adviser," Cosimo said swiftly. "My former tutor and your cousin's husband, John Fortune."

She supposed this was getting more dreamlike, for the man was nothing like she had read of the character of John Fortune, the strong, silent man of principle who had won Matilda's heart over the two princes who also desired her.

"I can see you've heard of me," said John Fortune smoothly. "But...you'll be hungry, come and eat."

For an instant, as Fortune held up the tent flap, Esther hesitated. But in the end, the smell of fire-cooked food was just too appealing. Her mouth began to water and she became aware that her stomach was rumbling. Even in dreams, one might as well be comfortable. She went in.

Seated on a hard wooden stool, she tucked into a bowl of thick, delicious broth. Fortune stood beside her with his hip leaning on the table, watching her with apparent indulgence.

Passing her some rough, sweet-smelling bread, he said, "I take it, since you are here, that you have come to help Matilda."

Esther took the bread and dipped it daintily into her soup. "Now why should you think that?"

It would have been simpler to say yes, but Esther was getting tired of passively agreeing to everything. Besides, now that her stomach had stopped complaining, curiosity was rising once again.

Fortune's eyebrows twitched. "For one thing, you've already annoyed Drago."

"I can't see how when we'd never met before this afternoon." She gave a quick, self-deprecating laugh. "Perhaps he just wanted my beautiful body."

Fortune didn't see the joke. He glanced over at Cosimo, a thoughtful expression in his eyes. "Perhaps he did."

"Would do no harm to have a back-up insider," Cosimo said. "In time. If the lady is willing."

Esther swallowed the soft, broth-soaked bread, glancing from one to the other. "To spy on Drago for you? Don't be ridiculous, I wouldn't go near him!"

"We need you," Fortune said, regarding her with a

31

disconcerting stare. "The people of Costanzo need you."

"Don't try and pull that one on me. You don't know me from Adam—or at least from Eve—and the people of Costanzo have even less idea who I am. I'm an interloper and I'll be gone...any time soon."

"Interloper?" Fortune repeated. "Interesting word."

"It's an interesting situation, but trust me, it's not going to last."

ω

They gave her a tent to sleep in all by herself, even sent a maid to help her prepare for bed. This dream seemed to be in real time, she thought, gazing at the pallet on which she was meant to spend the night, not episodic like any others she could remember. Well, maybe when she woke up, odd episodes were all she would remember from this one. Pity in its way...it was giving her a great feel for *The Prince of Costanzo.*

Which was another reason to wake up. If she was sleeping so long, she wouldn't have time to read the damned book, or any of the other stuff she needed to study. No way was Kevin going to miss this damned wedding. Or allow her to miss it.

What if this isn't a dream?

The idea hit her with a dull, uneasy lurch in her stomach.

Of course it's a dream! What the hell else could it be?

With sudden desperation she swung round on the departing maid whom she'd just dismissed with all the embarrassment of a modern woman faced with a servant.

"Wait a minute! Maria?"

"Madonna?"

Esther dragged her hand through her hair. She wanted the girl to say something incongruous and random and reassuringly dream-like. But obviously, she wouldn't speak unless Esther told her to.

"Why do they all hate Drago so much? What's wrong with him?"

"He's mad and evil, madonna."

"Where I come from, evil is a very strong word. What makes him evil?"

The girl came closer to whisper, "Magic, madonna. He uses dark magic."

Esther regarded her sceptically. The girl was sticking to the plot of the book—there was always something supernatural going on in those old Gothic novels. As far as Esther could remember Drago had murdered his father and his stepmother by some magical means, although there had been poison in the plot somewhere, too.

"To make the people love him?" she said, repeating Cosimo's accusation.

"Yes." Maria glanced over her shoulder. "And also women," she whispered. "They say he draws them into his castle and then does unspeakable things to them, and so besotted are they by means of his magic that they don't even object!"

"What sort of unspeakable things?" Esther asked with interest. "Torture?"

"Probably," said the girl dismissively. "But I mean—lustful things, fleshly things."

For some reason, the memory of the black-haired horseman insinuated itself, reminding Esther of his blazing eyes and sensual mouth and fit, strong body. Her own body began to tingle, and she wondered if it was going to turn into one of *those* dreams. Well, it wouldn't be surprising—she didn't get much action from Kevin.

"Hmm." She pulled herself together. "So, evil, lustful and master of the black arts. Clearly a bad thing."

The girl smiled with approval at her understanding.

"And Cosimo? He would make a better prince?"

"Oh yes, madonna," she said fervently. "Would you like me to undress you after all?"

"No thanks," Esther said hastily. "Good night."

When the girl had gone, she sat on the bed and waited, trying again to strain herself out of the dream. She tried pinching her arm till it was red. She tried bouncing up and down on the bed, but that achieved nothing except making herself giggle.

Now, she thought, would be an excellent time for a good book. *The Prince of Costanzo,* maybe.

Maria had brought her a fine linen night gown, but casting it to one side, Esther dragged the pins out of her hair and lay down on the narrow bed fully clothed, listening to the fading sounds of life around the camp as everyone bedded down for the night. Maybe if she fell asleep here, she would wake up back in the Hays' library. Before Hay woke her up and chucked her out for wasting his time. Maybe she was dribbling on his priceless book.

The camp grew silent, save for the eternal creaking of grasshoppers, the whine of the odd mosquito. How lifelike was that? She hoped the bites wouldn't itch beyond endurance.

Weird.

In fact, ridiculous. She was bored. What use was a dream of boredom? She could get that wide awake, with Kevin's friends at the weekend.

Bitch.

Well, damn it, I'm having a trying day. And night.

Abruptly, she sat up. There was no point in just lying there not sleeping. In fact, the urge just to go was strong. She had no idea how anyone—including the camp guards—would behave toward her, or where she would go, and she found the idea curiously exhilarating.

Shoving her feet back into her sandals, she pinned her hair back up with more enthusiasm than grace and walked quietly to the tent flap. It was easily untied. She even tied it again tidily behind her. All was quiet and still and very dark. The night was warm, a Mediterranean summer night. She stood for a moment taking in the brightness of the half-moon and stars in the black velvet sky; below it, the bodies stretched out around the camp. She moved forward carefully, gaze on the ground to prevent herself treading on anyone. Only once did she nearly come to grief when a dark-shrouded figure rolled over just as she was stepping across him. He landed on her foot and she had to be quite rough shaking him off. He snorted grumpily as she finally extracted herself, but didn't wake.

There were guards at the wooden gates who advised her politely to go back to bed.

"I can't," said Esther. "I need to pee—er—relieve myself. I'd rather do it outside the camp. I won't be long."

"Let me accompany you, madonna...."

"Certainly not!" Her genuine outrage must have communicated itself, because the guards said no more, simply opened the gate to her.

Of course, they might now tell Cosimo, but Esther didn't care. Something had to happen. And she had to go outside. Perhaps it was the path to waking.

Though the track was worn, it was difficult to keep to it in the dark. Her clothes snagged often on branches and thorns, and several times she felt scratches scrape down her arms and ankles, but she wouldn't stop. For some reason her heart beat like a rabbit's, welling with some unknown excitement.

And then she saw him. Ahead of her, at the end of the track, a shadowed horseman waited, silhouetted against the high grey hills. Instinctively, she halted, but her feet wouldn't let her pause. They dragged her forward. Curiosity was paramount now. She had to know...

He was watching her. As she drew closer, she thought she could even see his eyes glittering in the darkness. Impossible, but still she had the definite impression that those eyes were holding hers, drawing her onward to him. Because he was waiting for *her*.

"Halt there!" Abruptly, rough hands seized her, forcing her arms up behind her back. In front of her stood a second man, a soldier, who grabbed her by the chin, forcing her face up to the pale moonlight. "Name and password!"

"Esther and I don't know your stupid password. Let me go!" Wildly, she fought to escape, kicking out behind and in front, connecting with bone often enough and hard enough to draw muttered growls from her captors. Still they held on to her and she began to panic—not from personal fear so much as from a desire, a *need* to move forward, to reach the horseman.

Clearly the guards recognized her. Otherwise they would have thumped her long before sheer frustration drove the guard in front to draw back his fist purposefully. She was dragged back against the body of the other, whose foot swiped hers from under, leaving her momentarily helpless in face of the oncoming blow.

Before it came, the guard crumpled silently to the ground at her feet. A knife between his shoulder blades glittered in a shaft of moonlight. Shocked, Esther lifted her eyes to the dark figure who'd taken his place. The guard behind swore, pushing her away from him. Stumbling to her knees in the undergrowth, Esther saw the newcomer lunge forward, and then the second guard went down. An instant later, the dark shadow advanced on her. The moonlight glanced off his face, dark, handsome, bearded and familiar.

Drago.

Chapter Three

Esther scrabbled back into the undergrowth to get away from him, but he wasted no time, simply stretched forward, grabbed her by the hand and hauled her to her feet, dragging her on at once toward the end of the track.

The desperation she'd once felt to get there had totally vanished in the horror of violence and murder. Though it made no difference, she pulled back, straining against the implacable power of his steel-like grip. Behind her, she could hear movement, shouting. Cosimo's men were after her—or *him*...

Ahead of her, the dark horse still stood at the end of the track, impatiently shaking its head. Its rider had gone...

Of course he had. Drago had been its rider. Drago had been responsible for her compulsion to leave the camp, to get to him. It was all true. The man was a sorcerer.

But it doesn't matter. I'm dreaming! I'm dreaming!

Then why didn't she wake up? Dreams ended when the bad guy grabbed you, pushed you, touched you. You never got to feel his harsh grasp digging into your wrist, dragging you along the ground.

Desperately, she reached round with her free hand to claw at his fingers. But he simply swung her up in his arms like a sack of potatoes. The horse came dancing to meet them, and before she could get in even one blow, he shifted her into one arm and used the other to hoist himself into the saddle.

The horse leapt into motion like a released bullet, and Esther's struggling hands were suddenly clinging to Drago's cloak for safety. She glimpsed his face, exhilarated, excited, yet with a hint of grim determination in the set of his mouth. His glittering eyes roved restlessly, paying her no attention whatsoever.

For an instant, only her own grasp kept her secure as, with a screech of steel, her new captor drew his sword. She knew she was missing her chance of escape, but suddenly throwing herself off the galloping horse seemed as stupid as throwing herself out of a speeding car. And Drago hadn't drawn the sword to cut her throat, but to deal with an attack as several soldiers launched themselves at him from the side.

A clash of steel reverberated up his arm and through his body to her. She could feel his muscles rippling under her hand, against her side as he stabbed and hacked, and then they were free.

The horse had barely slowed at all, and now it lunged forward again at full speed. Drago, keeping his sword in his hand, at last spared her a glance. It was not comforting. There was wildness in the blazing, dark eyes that gave credence to accusations of insanity, a cruelty about the determined set of his sensual mouth that bore out just about everything else.

Curiosity, freedom from the camp were all very well, but delivering herself into this man's power was surely not the smartest move she'd ever made. Panic curled her fingers into fists around the fabric of his cloak and tunic. Wrenching his clothing, she pushed at the hard chest beneath.

"Stop! Let me go!"

A faint sound came from him. It might have been a breath of laughter. "Not yet." Steel scraped again as he replaced his sword in the scabbard dangling from his hip. Unexpectedly, his hand touched her head, causing her scalp to prickle in fear. An instant longer, his eyes bored into hers, reminding her of something, someone else, and gradually the expression in his eyes lost its wildness, became one of calm command.

Then his hand fell away, moving round her body to take the reins. The hypnotic gaze left her for the road ahead, and for some reason Esther felt the wind had been taken out of her sails. She had stopped struggling, her fists had already unclenched. Curiously, her fear had subsided. She remembered, as the rhythm of the horse beneath her grew increasingly familiar, that she was only dreaming. Horror at the brutality she had just witnessed began to lose its edge, and she realized she would just have to wait and see where this journey took her.

In the mean time, there was the heat of his arms around her body to soothe her, the hardness of his lean, fit body to rest against while the horse moved under them. It was oddly sensual, and she found herself secretly relaxing into the slow, lazy tingles of sexual sensation.

When, at last, sleep began to take her, she knew a pang of disappointment. Falling, she thought that now at last she was going to wake up, and knew a surprisingly strong pang of disappointment that she would never know the end of the dream.

ω

The sound of birds filled her ears, singing their hearts out in a medley both soothing and charming. Fresh, sweet-smelling air stirred her skin, soft comfort enfolded her body, brightness tugged at her eyelids.

Giving in, she cautiously opened her eyes. Not the Hay library. Bed. A large bed with posts and luxurious hangings in bright green and gold-embroidered fabric, on some sort of platform. The bed curtains weren't closed and she could see out to the open window from which came the freshness of the air and the bright, warm sun shining directly on her face. It was only a small window, though, and much of the spacious room was in shadow. Large tapestries hung on the walls, rugs were scattered about the wooden floor, adding depth and colour, but furnishings seemed sparse. A couple of carved wooden chests, an antique style porcelain wash basin and a large jug, a big wardrobe.

Something told her this was not the Hays' house. So where was she now? Had they taken her somewhere else while she slept? God forbid. Or was this another dream? How annoying was that when she hadn't finished with the old one?

Gingerly, Esther sat up. Which was when she made another discovery. She wasn't wearing her own clothes, but some sort of nightgown made of soft, fine linen. What's more, her hair was loose and there was no sign of her pins...

"She's awake," said a woman's voice with a mixture of warning and triumph. "Go and tell him."

A male grunt of acknowledgement followed, and as Esther twisted round, she was in time to see the door closing on a flash of blue fabric.

"How are you this morning?"

Slightly dazed, Esther gazed up at the speaker, a plump woman of middle years with a white cap on her head that tied under her chin. And a long dress of coarse fabric worn over some kind of under-dress that was visible top and bottom.

"Fine," she answered vaguely. "Thank you... I never thought I'd actually say this but—er—where am I?"

The woman chuckled. "Bless you, my lady, you're here in the prince's bed chamber."

"Prince's bed chamber! What prince?" As if it made a blind bit of difference. As if she didn't already know. It seemed the dream went on. Only this wasn't possible. This wasn't really a dream at all. She'd known it yesterday, but the alternatives were so impossible, so incomprehensible that she'd closed her eyes. It was easier to be asleep.

On the thought, she closed her eyes once more, but sleep stood no chance.

"Prince Drago, of course."

"And what the hell am I doing in his bed?"

"Bless you some more, my lady, you were sleeping like a baby when he brought you in. I suppose it seemed the easiest place to put you. Now don't look so outraged, for he never touched you."

"He didn't undress me, didn't sleep here?" Esther asked suspiciously, though why she'd got fixated on that issue rather than on the larger one she had no idea.

"Didn't sleep at all. He doesn't, very often. Now, just you calm down, young lady. The prince will answer all your questions when he comes in."

"Comes in?" Truly alarmed now, Esther seized the woman by the sleeve. "Look, you have to help me! He kidnapped me! Killed people. I think he even used some sort of mind-control to get me to him, then to make me sleep."

"Of course he did. Hush now..." the woman soothed.

Esther paused, staring at her kindly face. Slowly, she released the woman's sleeve. "*Of course he did*? You regularly take charge of his kidnap victims? What in Christ's name does he want with me?"

"You can ask him that yourself, dear."

"Oh no I can't." With determination, Esther threw back the bed covers and slid out of bed. It was unexpectedly high and her feet stumbled as she landed, slipping down the raised platform so that she fell painfully to her knees on the next step to the floor.

"I love to see a woman possessed of proper humility," said a male voice, one she recognized although it had said little enough to her, one that sent hot and cold shivers down her spine. Esther caught at her suddenly short breath, then grasped the bed post with both shaking hands to steady herself as she rose to face him.

"Now then, sir, don't go teasing her. She's confused enough as it is," said the woman.

He stood some feet away from her, head slightly on one side as he considered her. Shining black boots, some sort of leggings—hose?—that showed an alarming amount of strong, muscled leg, a dark red silk tunic, heavily embroidered in gold. From the tunic's round neckline emerged a snowy white shirt, made of fine pleated lace. His wild hair had been combed into order and he looked heart-stoppingly handsome as well as magnificent. Even the liquid dark eyes, though still frighteningly intense, had lost the wildness, the grimness of last night. Now they were still watchful, but curious, tinged with humour. And yet she had the impression that was all deliberate. His true thoughts were so deeply hidden you'd need a drill to penetrate them.

And where the fuck would I get a drill 'round here? Hysteria rose and had to be swallowed back down.

Drago said mildly, "Off you go, Lucrezia."

Lucrezia? Great. The nursemaid in the book, who does his every bidding. As she did now, bustling out of the room, though with various instructions and reprimands which Esther was too rattled to take in. In any case, Drago, still holding her defiant gaze, waved them away like a swarm of familiar flies.

His glance flickered to her trembling hand, which still held onto the bed post as to her only security. At once, she snatched it away, hiding it behind her back with the other one. Only then she felt ridiculously defenceless before him, wearing nothing but a loose nightgown that might have stretched to her ankles, but hadn't been properly laced up at the front. On their way back to her face, his eyes didn't linger there, but somehow she knew he was aware of it.

His full, sensual lips curved into a smile, a predatory cat finally cornering his victim.

"My lady," he said softly, dangerously. "How nice to see you again."

Esther swallowed, licked her dry lips. It took effort to meet his overwhelming gaze now, but she forced herself. "What do you want with me?" she demanded.

It wasn't conciliatory. She should have tried to pacify him, butter him up so he'd let her go, not piss him off even more...

He didn't look pissed-off—if she could judge from his face, which she doubted. Instead, his fading smile re-dawned.

"Isn't it obvious?"

Esther drew in her breath. "I'm too old and I'm crap in bed. What's more," she added with a spurt of inspiration, "I have syphilis."

A faint rush of laughter spilled over his lips and was gone. "Good try," he approved, strolling toward her. "But somehow, I don't believe any of these claims. However, though I'm sure your body contains many delights, they are not my first concern."

Stupidly, humiliation mingled with relief. And fear, although she refused to back away from him as her more cowardly instincts tried to insist.

He came to a halt in front of her, close but not touching, and gazed down into her face once more. "So tell me, strange lady, how *did* you get in here?"

Esther felt her eyes widen. Picking up her dropped jaw, she said, "You brought me! Apparently. I wouldn't know, being asleep at the time." She bit her tongue on the accusation that hovered. Suddenly it seemed ridiculous and childish to accuse him of making her fall asleep.

"Not this time," he said with such careful patience that she knew it was not inexhaustible. "The last time."

She stared at him. "The last time? I've never been here before in my life. I only...*arrived* yesterday in this...country."

"Don't lie to me," he said softly. It might have been the softness of a lover or an assassin. Either scared the pants off her. Or would have done if she'd been wearing any. "Don't you know who I am?"

"Drago," she managed. "Prince of Costanzo."

"You forgot bastard, insane, evil and sorcerer. Usurper and tyrant."

"What?" Wildly, she began to look around her for escape, though irresistibly her eyes were drawn back to his. They were opaque.

"When did you join my enemies?"

"I haven't joined anyone. I don't even want to *be* in this ridiculous place!"

His eyes searched hers, one to the other. Then, in a sudden movement that made her jump, he whirled round and sat on the step leading up to the bed. Head back against the bed post she had recently let go, he regarded her thoughtfully.

"Ever think you're mad?" he asked unexpectedly.

"Frequently. In the last twenty-four hours."

"Your name is Esther."

Warily, she inclined her head.

"When did you first see me, Esther?"

"Yesterday. Riding through that village…"

He sprang back to his feet with a sound of annoyance. Before she could even feel the panic, never mind get out of his way, he had her by the wrist, dragging her toward the door. Instinctively she tried to pull back, but it was pointless. He hauled her through another room, past more tapestries, stools and sofas and a large table, and then out into a corridor. By that time she decided that she was only hurting herself— literally—and stopped struggling.

He pulled her along the passage, past two gawping men dressed much in the same way as Drago though with less style, and up a narrow, spiral staircase to another passage. At the end of this, he flung open a door, dragged her inside and finally let her go. Her wrist smarted.

They were in a small, dark room with one single window high up in the right hand wall. A shaft of sunlight beamed onto the white pillows of the bed that was the room's only furniture. It smelled musty. Like a room that was never used or aired.

Uncertainly, she glanced up at Drago, who stood staring at her from the doorway. With curious deliberation, watching her the whole time, he moved past her, ripping off his tunic as he went, revealing the loose, white shirt beneath. It, too, he tore open until it gaped halfway down his powerful chest. Her heart thundered and yet for some reason she didn't run. Perhaps because he didn't touch her. Instead, throwing the tunic on the floor, he went and sat cross-legged on the bed.

Memory stirred, jolting her. Another male figure, sitting in the same pose, surely, on that same bed. An angry, grief-stricken boy who'd touched her heart even in the short moment of the dream. The first dream that she'd almost forgotten. Staring at this older man, she tried to smooth away ten years. Beneath the beard was the same beautiful bone-structure, the same slightly pointed chin. The same straight, arrogant nose. The same restless brown eyes, large and dark, not now liquid with sorrow but still recognizably his. She would have known them right away if she hadn't been so full of fear...

And, let's face it, the wild boy with the hint of danger had become a formidably frightening man.

Drago said, "Recognition dawns. Interesting."

He leapt off the bed as if it burned him, reaching down for his tunic in the same lithe movement.

Esther pulled her hair behind her head with both hands, twisting it. Then, lacking the pins, had to let it go again. She said weakly, "You've changed."

"But you haven't. Not one iota. That's even more interesting." As he spoke, he crossed the space between them, once more standing so close that she could feel the heat from his body. He smelled faintly of fresh herbs, which surprised her for some reason. "You are, I think, a sorceress. Did he teach you, too?"

"No...who?"

"Fortune."

Esther frowned. There was something here that she had to come back to. Struggling with it, she managed to say, "I thought you were a dream."

"That's what I thought of you when I tried to catch you and

you disappeared. You did much the same trick yesterday, although I presume it wasn't you who slaughtered my men in the process."

Distressed, Esther shook her head violently. "But you slaughtered theirs," she lashed out.

He shrugged, and the movement stirred the warm air around her body, making her tingle. "I doubt they're all dead."

"Don't you care?"

"No. I wanted you back."

"Why?"

His eyes darkened. "Since you were real, to find out how you got into my room ten years ago—and why. To learn your...arts." His gaze flickered downward, to the partial lacing over her breasts, to her waist and hips, and returned to her face, leaving her burning with a weird mixture of embarrassment, fear and excitement. Her nipples pressed against the thin shift. She prayed he hadn't seen.

"What arts?" she demanded. She wanted to run away from him, hide—at least find her clothes.

"You tell me."

"I have no arts. I shouldn't even *be* here. Hell, *you* shouldn't even be here!"

Swallowing another bout of hysterical laughter, she dragged her hand back through her hair, would have stepped away and left the room except that, at her first movement, he caught her wrist and jerked her back.

"You're not making sense."

"Do you imagine I don't know that?"

"Where have you come from, my strange lady?" His words were light, but his eyes bored into hers without pity. She felt a tug of compulsion, attraction, something she didn't understand but tried desperately to resist.

"You wouldn't believe me."

"Try me."

"No. I don't believe it myself."

"Do you know how beautiful you are?"

The unexpectedness took her breath away. Without permission, her gaze flickered down to his parted lips which, as he leaned down to her, were really too close for comfort.

She said flatly, "Crap."

His lips curved. She felt his breath of laughter on her mouth, almost like a kiss. *A kiss, my God, a kiss with* him? She couldn't breathe, couldn't move. Didn't want to, God help her.

"I knew I would like you, strange lady." His bent just a little closer. His mouth almost touched hers, then he smiled again and released her. "I have to be somewhere else. Come."

Bewildered, fighting a powerful emotion that she hoped was relief but felt suspiciously like pique or disappointment, she followed him out of the room and down the spiral staircase.

She wondered if it was the binding spell that Cosimo and John Fortune had gone on about. And Maria... Was Drago using it on her? She had no idea why he would do such a thing unless to extract her supposed knowledge. When the sad truth was, she had none. On the contrary, if she had to accept that this scary world was real and that she was alone in it, she knew less than anybody else.

She jumped as Drago's hand touched her shoulder, burning through the thin linen of her shift. But he only turned her to face the half-open door of his room and gently pushed.

"Lucrezia will help you dress. You and I will talk later."

She felt naked, bereft when his hand left her, stupidly more alone than ever. Without permission, her gaze followed him as he strode along the wide passage, his sword and dagger swinging at either hip. In front of him, a group of men parted and bowed, and one of them began to walk with him. Drago flung an arm around his shoulder as they walked, but didn't reduce his speed. They disappeared together 'round the corner, and Esther, not knowing what else to do right now, went into Drago's room.

Lucrezia bustled about immediately, giving another woman swift directions while she led Esther back into the bed chamber off the outer room, which seemed to be a mixture of private office and sitting room. Numbly, Esther let them carry on.

Denying all knowledge of Esther's own clothes, Lucrezia gave her instead a light cream underdress and a heavier linen overdress in a rather lovely shade of green, both of which the other maid brought in and displayed like a prize, clearly expecting Esther to be pleased. To Esther, gazing with longing at the open window, it seemed far too much to wear in this heat, but if she could just get out of here to *think*, then she could get rid of one or other of them...and the sleeves— sleeves!—that they insisted on fastening on to the whole ensemble, all folds and ruches and ribbons. Ugh.

They even brushed her hair, leaving it largely loose, but fastening a wispy veil to the top of her head. It felt very strange. She'd worn it up since she was fifteen. Jenny, her sister, had often demanded to know why she didn't just cut it.

At least she wouldn't get sunburn.

Released from their tender mercies, she moved at once to the window and looked out into the warm sunshine.

The view was stunning. She seemed to be in a castle, more like a fairy-tale fantasy than the rough, stark ruins she was used to seeing. It stood on the top of a hill, and if she stuck her head right of the window and twisted upward, she could see towers and turrets reaching into the unrelieved blue sky. The dragon banner she'd seen with Drago's soldiers flew from one of them. Not surprising: Drago meant dragon.

Below her stretched endless, lush green hills and valleys, each rolling into the next with spectacular beauty. Small villages and fields were scattered among them. The tiny specs of people and animals moving through them seemed more imagined than real.

And directly below her, an ornamental courtyard lined by arches leading into a covered area. Exotically dressed men and women moved through it, like representatives of some alien, brightly coloured species, calling to each other or sitting in the shade to gossip.

Though it seemed to be early morning still, the sun beat hotly down on Esther's face, on the top of her head. For some reason, that distinctive sensation did more than anything else to convince her of the reality of this place she had somehow stumbled into.

Almost shocked, she recognized excitement growing in among the terror. Drago was *real*; he was the boy who'd moved her in that first dream, that first, brief visit...

No one stopped her leaving Drago's quarters. The servants and other curious, more gorgeously dressed people she encountered on the way merely moved out of her way with a bow. Of course, she had no idea where she was going, but despite the unexpected charm of discovering herself in an antique palace, Esther grimly plodded on until she found herself in a huge entrance hallway with large double doors. Sunlight gleamed beguilingly from the tiny spaces under and around the doors, but they were guarded by a large servant. Esther marched forward determinedly, her heart thundering as she wondered how to make the man let her outside.

In the end it was easy. The man opened the door for her without a word—and she could walk into the light, feel the faint breeze stir her hair while the strong sun beat down on her head. In something of a daze, she instinctively left the main drive, crossing the lawn and the gardens toward what looked like a perimeter fence.

It was a wooden rail that ran around the edge of the castle grounds. Below was a spectacular view over a vast countryside of hills, rivers and fields. It made Esther dizzy just to look.

Hastily, she stepped back and sank down on a wooden bench from where she could admire the view without vertigo. Only she no longer saw the scenery; her head was spinning.

She had no idea how any of this was possible. She was living in the world of the book, *The Prince of Costanzo*, only it was later in the story and everything was just a little different...*he* was just a little different.

But did it truly make any difference that he was the beautiful boy? Did it make him less of a villain? The boy had been angry, had frightened her by lunging, and yet she had sensed no real threat from him. But the man? That was much more questionable. And if she was living in this world, so many things were possible—evil magic, supernatural murders...

It was dizzying. In fact, she felt so dizzy now, she was afraid of falling off her bench. Grasping the edges, she tried to will herself not to faint as the world began to close in and spin. Something dragged her down into the darkness with irresistible force. Everything swayed and swung and stupidly she was furious because she knew that after all she'd been wrong, and now, at last she was about to wake up in reality.

Chapter Four

The world righted itself and steadied. Disoriented, breathless, Esther sat at the big mahogany desk, her arms flopped in her lap. In front of her eyes, open on the table, lay *The Prince of Costanzo*. It must have fallen out of her hands and the jolt had woken her up.

With wonder, she dropped her gaze to her knees, taking in the brightness of her familiar, colourful skirt. No heavy, exotic gowns trailed to her ankles.

But what a dream...

Her hand trembled as she drew it across her face and through her hair. It wasn't just vivid, it was...like a vision. Was Margaret Marsden's writing truly as brilliant as all that?

Or was it so dull it had sent her to sleep, to dream of something more interesting?

And yes, it *was* interesting. Drago was interesting. Just thinking of him made her skin tingle, sent butterflies gamboling about her stomach.

Even if he had murdered his own father.

Almost involuntarily, she reached out again for the book. Then she snatched her hand back. She needed a break, a reality check.

And who better for keeping her feet on the ground than

Kevin? Grabbing her phone from her bag, she stood, keyed his number and walked across to the window while it connected. Her legs felt stiff, as if they'd run a half-marathon and then seized up while she sat still for too long.

As if she'd walked a long way through the hills and woods, been bumped through rough country on the back of a horse and then slept for hours in warm, soft bed...

"Hello?"

Kevin's slightly peeved voice dispelled the returning vision. "Hi Kevin, it's me. What are you up to?"

"Nothing. There's nothing *to* get up to around here, is there?"

"Well, that's one reason I'm phoning," Esther soothed, squashing her own irritation. "We've been invited for drinks tonight with Sir Ian and Lady Hay."

She smiled ruefully as she heard his breath catch. Hopefully, this would make up for being here. "They're having a drinks party, I gather, but we don't have to be formal. If you'd like to go," she added for devilment.

"Nothing better to do, have we?" he said briskly. "I'm sure it will be lovely. Did you accept?"

"No, I said you hated this dump of a village and had no intention of associating with the ridiculous yokels."

"Esther!"

She sighed. "I'm kidding, Kevin." Why did she have to explain this after a relationship of three years?

"Very funny." Clearly, he was too excited about tonight to be really angry. Esther had broken the connection and was walking back to the desk before it struck her that he had never once asked if *she* wanted to go.

The temptation now was to read *The Prince of Costanzo*, but she really couldn't risk wasting all her research time in sleep—how *could* she have slept instead of reading? Twice! She hesitated over the envelope containing story notes—a chaotic jumble of scribbles—but in the end decided she was obsessed enough with Margaret's stories for the time being and instead took out some letters written by Margaret's husband.

Laying most of them aside, she decided to concentrate first on those relating to the illness which led up to Margaret's disappearance and death. Those she placed precisely on top of the still open *Prince of Costanzo*, just in case her eyes strayed back to that fascinating world.

A phrase in the first letter caught her eye at once. "My wife is very taken with him..."

Esther's heart began to beat faster. The lingering fringes of the dream burned away as her quest to find a lover for Margaret took over. Surely she could at least make an inspired guess about the mystery if there was true love in the picture. For from all she had read so far, Margaret's marriage had not been one of mutual love. She had married above her, and her writing, which she had begun before her marriage, had become increasingly an escape from the constant reminders of her inferior birth. Her husband the earl seemed a rather aloof figure, initially besotted with his bride, but soon regarding her as more of an embarrassment. Not only was she unsuited to be a great nobleman's wife, but she wrote "silly Gothic romances". Worse than all, word of her identity got out, and the earl put his foot down. No more writing, no more books. And Margaret went into some sort of decline.

The letter held in front of her was written by the earl to a Lady Butler, dated April 1817, thanking her for recommending a physician with a Russian looking name. The earl's handwriting was not particularly clear at that point, but it looked like Doctor Nelurof, or Nelorof perhaps. Anyway, despite the earl's scepticism, Margaret had apparently brightened after his first visit, and the earl had asked him to call again the following day.

Intrigued, Esther began to search for further references to Nelurof, but could find none. What she did find were two more of the earl's letters, both written on the same day in May 1817. The first mentioned casually that Margaret was much improved, "a little over-bright perhaps" but almost returned to normal. The second, written that evening, stated she did nothing but sleep.

So which was it, Esther wondered, frowning to herself. It almost sounded as if Margaret alternated between feverish liveliness and long periods of exhaustion. As she put the letters away, the pages of the book beneath got ruffled and flicked back to the title page and frontispiece. A portrait of Margaret Marsden looked back at her, painted while she was Countess of Hawton. Young, dark and pretty, she looked both elegant and tragic. Her eyes opened wide into the "camera" and yet they gave the impression of being somewhere else, of secret thought, a secret life. A lot of writers looked like that, Esther reflected, at least some of the time...

The Prince of Costanzo was the last book she had published. The date on the title page was 1817. It must have been one of the very few ever distributed, for the earl had had them recalled and destroyed. Paid sweetly for it, too, according to contemporary rumour.

Irrelevantly, Esther wondered what she would have done in Margaret's place. For women then, things were different. If Kevin ever got beyond merely reviling her writing and tried to forbid it, she would have no difficulty telling him what to do with his orders, and she would be quite within her rights to do so. Margaret, however, leaving aside her upbringing and centuries of custom, would have had considerable legal difficulty if she'd try to defy her husband. And of course, he was her own and her family's financial security.

Would that have mattered to Margaret? Was it that or her children that kept her with the earl? Slowly declining into depression and illness. Did she escape—leaving her children behind after all—and find love? With the Russian doctor? No real reason to think so. Perhaps she'd been right earlier and Margaret simply slid into catalepsy and died. The depression, the "decline", however, appeared to have been real.

Having married a man she didn't love, for duty, would she have had the courage to leave her husband? Would she, Esther, have the courage to leave Kevin if he had the power to stop her writing?

Courage...would it be *courage* to leave Kevin? Did she really love writing more than her fiancé? That felt uncomfortable. So did the weird feeling of freshness when she thought about starting anew. She couldn't imagine life without Kevin now, but she wasn't afraid of it.

Slightly shocked by the turn of her thoughts, she asked herself if she still loved Kevin. There were times when they irritated the hell out of each other, when they were poles apart in thought, spirit, opinion. Yet they were still together. Didn't that count for something?

It had to. And she understood Kevin so well that it didn't really matter that he had never understood her. And yet the spark had gone. In fact, since meeting Drago, dreaming the dream, she doubted it had ever been there. But even dreaming, the emotion inspired by Drago couldn't be dignified by the description *love*; it had been half fear and half animal attraction.

And she couldn't live her life comparing it to a dream, however strange and however vivid. Deliberately, she glanced at her watch. Five o'clock!

Hastily, she scribbled a few notes on her pad and closed the book, laying it down on the top of her unread pile. That done, she grabbed her bag and jacket and left.

ω

"What are you doing?" Kevin demanded. "Why aren't you ready?"

Esther jumped guiltily. Sprawled on the bed in her towel, she had her laptop on the pillow and was Googling all possible forms of Doctor Nelurof's name. There had been nothing under either Nelurof, Nelurov, Nelorof or Nelorov. Thinking how often people forgot to cross their t's, she had just hit the search button for Neturof when Kevin interrupted.

He was smartly dressed in a light, casual suit, freshly combed and shaved. He would have looked handsome if he hadn't been frowning so irritably. Had he always looked this peevish?

"I *am* ready," Esther insisted lightly. "I just have to sling my clothes on. Everything else is done. I'm just checking something..."

She glanced at the screen without much hope. Two results had come up. She clicked on the first one. An entry in an on-line biographical dictionary.

"Neturof, Doctor Ivan, active c. 1816-1818. Poss. Russian origin. Practiced in London among the fashionable upper classes. His methods were unorthodox and mysterious, but he seems to have cured many maladies from toothache to tuberculosis. Ellen, Lady Butler is known to have recommended him to all her friends following the cure of her son's suspected consumption, although other physicians cast doubt on the original diagnosis. After 1818, he disappears from record."

"Wow!" Esther murmured, pressing the back button and clicking on the second article. "This is amazing! Margaret's doctor seems to have disappeared round about the same time as she did. Is that coincidence or is that coincidence?"

"Esther, for God's sake," Kevin fumed. "Are we going to this party or not?"

It was on the tip of Esther's tongue to say she'd rather stay here and research further, but when she thought of Kevin's disappointment at losing this, his only treat out of her day of wonder, she immediately gave in.

"Sorry." She closed the laptop lid, and slid off the bed. "Getting carried away again. Won't be a minute..."

ω

Esther was quite surprised by the warmth of Lady Hay's welcome. There was something more than social grace in her smile and she did seem genuinely determined to catch up with them later as she promised. As they moved into the drawing room, where the majority of guests had gathered, Kevin regarded her with a pride that had been noticeably absent in recent months.

Once, this would have pleased her. For some reason it only annoyed the hell out of her tonight. She really couldn't see what there was to be proud about, just because a middle-aged lady was friendly toward her. Lots of people were friendly to her. Perhaps she was pre-menstrual, because Kevin's snobbery was beginning to seem a less lovable flaw by the minute.

Music played in the background, too quietly to disrupt

conversation. It sounded like jazz. Sir Ian Hay was standing with his back to an impressive fireplace, talking to a prosperous looking middle-aged couple and a younger man. He saw them arrive, though, for through a gap in the clusters of guests, he lifted his glass in a toast of silent welcome. He even made a movement as if he meant to leave his companions and come and greet them. Fortunately, Kevin missed this, and in any case, Lady Hay appeared unexpectedly, asking what they would like to drink. Two minutes later, armed with charged glasses, they stood in a little cluster of their own while Kevin explained his job to Lady Hay.

Well, she asked. She can't complain.

But she could, Esther discovered, turn the subject rather more adroitly than anyone else she had encountered.

"My goodness," she exclaimed in one of Kevin's tiny pauses for breath. "You are both such clever people. Esther was telling me about her book, too—I was so impressed... I have to tell you, Esther, I made a gaff letting you come without proper vetting. My husband was most displeased with me—until he met you, of course. You can tell at once, sometimes, if a person is on the level, as it were. I told him you clearly were, but of course he didn't believe me until he spoke to you for himself. He appreciates the way you value this part of his collection."

"You don't share his enthusiasm for book collecting?" Esther asked. She already knew the answer, but she had to say something before Kevin turned the conversation back to himself. And she noted she was now addressed by her first name—a mark of approval certainly not lost on her fiancé.

Lady Hay smiled. "No, I'm afraid I don't. Don't get me wrong, I read a lot, but putting dusty and often ugly old books in cabinets just does nothing for me. Of course it's not just the books, it's all the paraphernalia that goes with them, relating to the authors, publishers, individual editions...makes me go cross-eyed! I collect other things, very different to my husband's tastes."

She smiled and lifted one hand to delicately caress the diamond and peridot pendant at her throat. "Jewellry," she explained. "Antique jewellry. Which is why I was so taken with your ring, Esther."

Instinctively, Esther spread her hand, as if to check the ring was still there.

Lady Hay said, "There it is! Don't you think that's the most beautiful thing you've ever seen?"

Kevin, who had often expressed gratitude that Esther didn't wear it on her left hand and make anyone think he had given her such a tawdry old thing for their engagement, smiled and murmured obediently, "Very beautiful indeed."

"I don't suppose," Lady Hay suggested, almost apologetically, "that you would consider selling it to me?"

Ah. So that is the root of the new friendliness! Poor Kevin...

"I'm sorry, I couldn't sell it. It's a family thing."

Lady Hay sighed. "I know, you explained yesterday. Obviously, I respect that... I would give you a very good price though, which is quite a consideration for two people starting out together. It would pay for your wedding, or a damn good honeymoon. Deposit on a house..."

The light of genuine lust gleamed in their hostess's eyes as they flickered from their faces to the ring. She gave a hopeful smile and in spite of her cynicism, Esther's heart warmed to her.

"I'm flattered you like it so much, but I can't. I really can't part with it."

Kevin's foot came down heavily on her toes, making her

suppress a wince. "Let us think about it for a little," he said winningly, and Lady Hay brightened, giving him one last assessing glance before she smiled and excused herself to greet some new arrivals.

"Why did you say that?" Esther hissed. "I've no intention of selling it!"

"Well maybe you should re-think your intentions. Did you not grasp the sort of money she's talking about here?"

"Money isn't everything."

"No, but it helps to buy little things like houses. Or a decent-sized wedding."

Esther's parents, retired and increasingly vague academics, were happy to pay for the wedding. But their plans—which were in fact Esther's wishes—were on a much smaller scale than Kevin's ambitions. As a result, it was a long time since either of them had spoken about the wedding. They didn't even have a date for it.

Esther's breath caught. Smiling at a couple as they squeezed past, she murmured, "Do we have to talk about this now?"

"Yes! She's made her offer now and we'd be fools to let it slip away. Unless—you're hoping she'll bid higher?"

Esther almost screamed. It was on the tip of her tongue to say she was heading back to the village before her head exploded, but the very next person who stopped to talk to them was Sir Ian Hay.

He made jovial small talk for a minute or two before asking Kevin if he shared Esther's enthusiasm for Gothic literature. Kevin had to confess that this was not his main strength. Before he could expound on what his strengths actually were, Hay had already turned to Esther, asking how her research was coming along.

"Pretty well, actually. I've discovered loads of stuff that I haven't even sniffed at anywhere else."

"It's a unique collection," Hay agreed, "and not normally available for consultation. Few people know of its existence. And then Marsden was a minor writer, even within the Gothic genre, and no one has yet written a book devoted to her. You are the first. And yours will be fiction."

His tone didn't make it clear whether he found that disappointing or not. Esther said ruefully, "To be honest, I'm wondering now if I couldn't do both. I think there's a wonderful story in there..."

"Quite a sad story," Hay pointed out.

"Well, maybe not. Or only in some ways. I came across an interesting name today, a doctor called Neturof..."

Hay's gaze, which had been scanning the room, now came quickly back to her. "Neturof," he repeated softly.

"That's right, and the *really* interesting thing is, he seems to have disappeared from the world at about the same time as Margaret. I'm wondering if they aren't connected in some way. Certainly it's an idea for fiction."

"It might even be true. Unfortunately we have no way of knowing..." His eyes grew speculative as they looked into hers. "...I imagine... And have you read *The Prince of Costanzo*?"

"Not yet. I'm hoping to have time tomorrow."

"Oh? I thought I saw you reading it this afternoon. Mind you, I didn't think you could be enjoying it much, because when I stuck my head in the library, you were asleep."

Esther's heart jolted. Asleep, and dreaming...

Warm blood suffused her face. It was humiliating enough to be caught asleep while researching. She could only hope she hadn't snored. "I did nod off at one point," she confessed. "I've no idea why. I *never* sleep during the day, and I'm desperate to read *The Prince*."

"I did hear a rumour of some strange effects of that particular book, but to me, it was just another novel—and not even her best work. Her villain was good, though. I'd say *he's* one of the best of the genre."

"Drago." Saying the name gave her the strangest thrill, like repeating a word normally forbidden. It conjured him up in her mind's eye, his lean, hard body close to hers, his wild, intense eyes burning yet teasing, his breath warm on her lips...

Swallowing, she said, "What makes him so good a villain?"

"Not sure. Perhaps because in many ways he's a likeable chap, but unafraid to use every dirty trick in the book to attain his goal of power. One of the best charismatic villains I've read."

If he was like her dream, then she had to agree. She said weakly, "Must get to it tomorrow... I meant to ask you, too, do you have any more material relating to Neturof? Even stuff unconnected to Margaret?"

For an instant, he regarded her impassively. His gaze flickered across the room—to his wife who, interestingly, seemed to be keeping an eye on them, too.

"Come to the library," he said abruptly. "No one will miss us for a few minutes."

Esther rather thought Lady Hay would, for she felt her gaze following them as she left the room with her host, Kevin trailing after them slightly bewildered.

The library was in darkness when Hay pushed open the door. He switched on one light in the centre of the room, which cast a pale, shadowy glow around the rows of books and the tall, covered windows.

"Neturof is a rather mysterious figure," Hay said, wandering across to a glass bookcase at the back of the room. He delved into his pocket and came up with a collection of small keys, one of which he used to unlock the glass door in front of him. "Interested, it seems, in the occult as much as in traditional medicine."

"Really? What makes you believe that?"

"Well...some of his books have come into *my* collection. Books he owned rather than books he wrote. Like this one for example."

He took a leather bound, quarto-sized book from the shelf and showed the spine to Esther and Kevin. The leather was very old, but in good condition, and pressed in gold lettering across the spine was *Secrets of Necromancie.*

Hay pressed it into her hands. "Open it."

Obediently, wondering where this was going, Esther held the book, spine supported in her palm, and opened it at the title page. The paper was still surprisingly white and clear against the black print of the lettering, some in bold, some italics.

"Secrets of Necromancie, Discovered and Revealed by John Fortune. Printed privately at his Presse, in this Year of Our Lord 1571."

Esther closed her mouth. "John Fortune? Isn't that the name of the English hero in *The Prince of Costanzo*?"

"Yes it is. Which makes me wonder if Margaret Marsden did not know Neturof before he attended her as a physician. Of course it's just a name, and John Fortune in the book is about the only character who *doesn't* practice magic. But it is a coincidence."

"Perhaps she just liked the sound of the name," Esther said lightly. But a memory was plucking at her mind. Drago, standing close to her...

"You are, I think, a sorceress. Did he teach you, too?"

"No...who?"

"Fortune."

Her dream was not Margaret's story...but where the hell was it coming from?

"Put it with your other materials for tomorrow," Hay said.

"Really? Don't you want it locked away?"

"As I said, my main security is secrecy. Very few people know what I have. My only request to you is that you maintain my privacy—no acknowledgments in your book, and no sending your friends here. As Professor MacGowan did with you."

"No problem," Esther said faintly, making a mental note to thank that old family friend most heartily for telling her about this place. She closed the book, and Hay, his gaze on her right hand, said, "That is an extraordinarily beautiful ring. I expect my wife has already made you an offer for it."

"I had to tell her I wasn't selling." Beside her, Kevin made a silent shuffle of protest.

Hay smiled. "Tell you what...I've just given you even more to read for tomorrow. If you want to take half an hour now, I'll cover for you at the party. If you like."

"Really?" Esther couldn't believe her luck.

Hay laughed. "Really." And when Esther glanced at Kevin, he added, "Kevin and I will go and discuss business things, and collect you back here."

Naturally, Kevin saw nothing wrong with this arrangement, which, perversely, irritated Esther. However, while the men walked out of the room, she was already sitting down at the desk, laying John Fortune's book carefully down in front of her. It might be interesting, she thought, to see if there was any of Fortune's book in *The Prince*...

Slowly, she reached for *The Prince of Costanzo* and picked it up. The urge to open it was overwhelming, almost like the dream-compulsion to leave Cosimo's camp. She tried to laugh at herself, but couldn't. She really couldn't be afraid of falling asleep, of falling back into the dream...

Taking a deep breath, she opened the book.

The print rushed up to meet her, dark and jumbled, dragging her inward. There was no time to resist, or even to fear. Around her, the darkness spun, pushing her into the spiral of the book and spitting her out with a jolt.

Chapter Five

Brightness stung at her eyes. For an instant, she thought she was still falling, for everything was a long way down: a rough road and the rolling hills beyond, and brightly dressed riders talking and laughing as they made their leisurely way up the winding track.

She was back where she'd fallen asleep in the last "dream". God, this was weird....

Blinking away the dizziness, Esther rose from her wooden bench and moved forward to grip the wooden rail and gaze downward. Men and women rode together. A few men held great birds on their thickly gloved hands. Falcons. It was a hunting party. And in the midst, in dark red short cloak and hat, she recognized Drago. Like the sun, he rode steadily onward, saying little but smiling amiably enough as his satellites moved about him on horseback, talking, laughing, gesticulating, swapping places and positions as complicated as a country dance, in never-ending bids for the prince's attention.

As he rode out of the castle's shadow into the glaring sun, it seemed to Esther that he shone brighter. For an instant, his face was guileless, so beautiful that it caught at her breath. And then, as if he sensed her, his head twisted and he looked upward, directly at her.

Instinctively, Esther fell back out of his sight, and stumbled into someone solid behind her. Firm hands gripped her arms briefly, steadying her. She looked up into the craggy, weather-worn face of a still young man. Piercing, intelligent hazel eyes gazed back at her, half-teasing, half-curious.

"The lady Esther if I mistake not. At last."

"At last?" she repeated vaguely. He was more plainly dressed than the riders below, or any men but servants that she had seen around the castle, but his manner was authoritative, a man used to being obeyed.

"Before he rode out, the prince bade me look after you and show you the castle. You seem to have managed well enough without me."

Since she had no idea whether she had or not, Esther didn't answer. She was wearing the dress Lucrezia had given her, not her own clothes, which was interesting, but she had no idea how much time had passed since she'd first sat on the bench. Half an hour, a week, or ten years...?

"Who are you?" she asked bluntly. *Jailer, nurse-maid, spy...?*

"Arturo di Ripoli, Captain of the Army of Costanzo, at your service." *Apparently the former.*

As he stepped back to a more conventional distance, the threat lessened, and Esther let herself look up at the amazing building behind him. They were in a formal garden, neatly kept, full of tall roses and brightly coloured flowers Esther didn't recognize. Behind this, the high stone walls of the castle rose, stark but beautiful. There was only one turret from this angle. Esther felt it should house Rapunzel or some other princess in need of rescue. Maybe that's where the captain was escorting her.

Well, she'd been curious to come back. *Go with the flow, Esther*

Following the civil gesture of his hand, she consented to walk forward. Vaguely aware of the different terminology of bygone days, she said lightly, "Does this mean you are an officer of the army, or that you command it?"

"That I command it. Under the prince."

Well, that would account for the authority. "And is it a large army you command? A—busy one?"

"Larger and busier than it used to be," came the slightly grim answer.

Esther regarded his serious face curiously. "Because of Cosimo? So he is a genuine threat to the prince?"

"He's more of a threat to the people."

"In what way?"

Arturo shrugged. "He requisitions their crops and animals to feed himself and his mercenaries, billets undisciplined soldiers on them, brings fear where there was none before—"

"I saw some of that fear," Esther interrupted, remembering the scattering of people from the village street when she had first "arrived". "It was fear of Drago, not Cosimo."

"Cosimo taught them to fear the prince. With lies."

Lies? Come on, I may not have read the book, but I know what's in it!

Only this wasn't quite the same as the book, was it? This was a future story, based on a changed ending for the previous one. In this scenario, not Cosimo but Drago was victorious. And Cosimo was reduced to invading and living off the people.

"I take it you are a loyal follower of Prince Drago," she said, not troubling to keep the cynicism out of her voice. She may not have been dreaming in the accepted sense, but right now she found it very hard to grasp that this world was real in any way.

Arturo's eyebrow twitched at her tone. "Of course."

"Why 'of course'? Didn't he usurp the power his father intended for Cosimo?"

"Prince Rudolfo had no right to do that. Drago was his heir."

"Drago is illegitimate."

Arturo sighed. "You have been listening too trustfully to Cosimo. Drago is perfectly legitimate."

Not in the book, he isn't!

Okay, complete script change—why do I even try to understand what's going on?

"Then why did Rudolfo pass him over? Was he unsuitable in some other way?"

Arturo gave her a slightly sly smile. "Perhaps he, too, listened too trustfully to Cosimo."

Esther gave a reluctant laugh and allowed herself to be led into the next garden, which contained hedges and walkways, leading into a taller maze. Wooden benches had been set under the shade of trees, and from one of these, Esther saw the hunting party return to the castle in a blaze of noise and colour. Gorgeously dressed men and women vied for the prince's attention, the younger ones trying to draw him into some game.

But the prince merely dismounted among them, threw the reins to the waiting boy and, waving the people away like a swarm of flies, leapt up the steps into the castle's great entrance way. Esther wasn't sure if she was piqued or relieved by being unnoticed.

"Clearly, it's a hard life being the prince," Esther observed. "Who are all these people?"

"Some of the nobility of Costanzo."

"Where are the rest? With Cosimo?"

"A few," Arturo admitted. "Others are simply at home ruling

71

their lands. Court life isn't to everyone's tastes."

"It appears to be to Drago's."

Arturo smiled vaguely. "Some of it," he agreed. It wasn't a satisfactory answer. None of his answers were, though she wasn't quite sure what she wanted to hear. Restlessly, she stood again.

"What will he do now? Nap before dinner?"

"Oh no. It's justice time. And then petitions. And a state meeting. I don't know what else."

"Justice time?" Esther repeated suspiciously, ideas of summary executions and floggings filling her with dread. Drago had been a cruel tyrant in the book.

"Largely minor local disagreements," Arturo said dismissively. "Although we do have one traitor. Would you like to see the court at work? We can sit at the back."

"All right." Her heart beat faster. Without noticing, she had sunk into it again: the "dream" was as real as life. "Who is your traitor?" she asked, as Arturo led her farther around the castle.

"Alessandro de Verini. He recently inherited land in the west. Chose to support Cosimo against us and was captured in a skirmish."

"What will happen to him?"

"That's what will be decided."

The courtroom was a hall inside the castle, accessed from a side door. A couple of noblemen and women sat at the back already, a splash of luxurious colour among the sea of plain and drab dress surrounding them—the ordinary folk who made up the vast majority of the crowded room. A soldier stood idly by the door exchanging banter with a young peasant girl, although he sprang to attention at sight of Arturo.

"Is it always this busy?" Esther asked as she and Arturo

took their places on a hard wooden bench. The noisy folk, mostly chattering or laughing or even throwing things to each other, did not look like cowed subjects. Perhaps they were the sort who enjoyed public executions.

"Not always," Arturo answered. "I suspect a lot of them are drawn by the traitor Alessandro de Verini. More of a spectacle than the usual missing chickens and drunk and disorderly behaviour."

A soberly dressed man clutching a sheaf of papers and books bustled in from an internal door near the platform, which he strode onto, laying his burden on the table there and sorting through it. Behind the table stood a large, almost thronelike high-backed chair.

There seemed little doubt as to who would sit there.

The busy man jumped down to a smaller table in front of the platform and made a fuss about laying out book and quill. After which he stood rigidly to attention—and as if by magic, the babble of the courtroom died away to nothing.

Immediately into the silence strode Prince Drago, without his hat now, but otherwise still in the dark red he had been wearing at the hunt—and in her earlier meeting with him before she went to sleep, went back, whatever it was she did... Perhaps that really had been just *this* morning...

Everyone stood, including Arturo. Esther remained defiantly seated. But Drago seemed quite unconcerned about making an entrance, simply strode to the high-backed chair and sat impatiently waving the populace to sit, too. They did, still in silence.

Drago glanced at the paper in front of him on the table, then looked up and scanned the court. Esther was sure he saw her. Certainly, he acknowledged Arturo with a twitch of his eyebrow, but he made no greeting or gesture of surprise to see her there. Instead, his gaze moved smoothly on into the crowd.

Apparently he found the face he was looking for, because he frowned over his fixed stare and said abruptly, "Giuseppe, have you returned that damned chicken yet?"

A round-shouldered individual stood, shuffling his feet, twirling a dirty hat between nervous fingers. The courtroom held its collective breath, and Esther wondered wildly if in this world you died for stealing chickens.

"Er—no, my lord..."

"Why not?" barked the prince.

"I—er..."

"He ate it, my lord," piped up a feminine voice, and the court erupted into laughter at this, the punchline they had presumably been waiting for. "He'd eaten it before the last hearing, but he was too feared to tell you."

Drago's lip seemed to twitch. Even Arturo was chuckling to himself.

Drago said sternly, "Then Guiseppe, you give Pietro three of your own before sun-set today. And to make sure, Messire Dandalo here will choose the three and deliver them. And Giuseppe, if I ever see you here again, I'll lock you up. Federico!"

In something of a daze, Esther watched him go through a series of minor law infringements in much the same way, and declare his judgment on a disputed strip of land. His only harsh punishment was of a man who had got drunk and beaten his wife and children. This individual was barred from the village tavern and sentenced to be flogged.

After the almost light-hearted proceedings that had gone before, this case and its punishment numbed Esther. And before she could recover, Drago moved on. They were still dragging the unfortunate drunkard out of the court, when Drago said impatiently, "Bring in Alessandro de Verini."

Even the downtrodden woman crying over the fate of her brutal husband stopped snivelling as the next prisoner was brought in.

Unarmed, but unchained either, Alessandro de Verini walked into the room between two soldiers, every inch the nobleman. His clothes were fine, if a little dusty and ripped up one sleeve. He carried himself like a prince. And of course the overall impression was helped by the fact that he was young and handsome.

Led to the dock—a bar across the floor to one side of the platform—he looked up at Drago with defiance in his closed face. You could have heard a pin drop in the courtroom.

Drago nodded, almost as if they were meeting socially. "Alessandro."

The young man simply stared back at him.

"Alessandro, you stand before me accused of combining with my enemies against the sovereign prince and people of Costanzo. How do you plead?"

"Not guilty," said Alessandro clearly.

Drago sat back in his chair. He began to look bored. "And yet you were captured with the foreign forces of my cousin Cosimo, were disarmed trying to hack two of my officers into pieces while shouting, 'Death to Drago'. Sounds guilty to me."

Alessandro lifted his chin. "I don't deny any of those things. What I deny is your right to be called sovereign or prince. What I deny is any guilt of treason against a usurper!"

There was a faint hiss of indrawn breath around the courtroom now. All eyes turned on the prince with avid if fearful expectation.

Drago yawned.

"You know," he said conversationally, bringing his eyes back to the prisoner, "Cosimo must have jumped for joy on finding you. It must have been like taking candy from a baby. How much silver did you give him? Did you hand over your entire lands, or just let him ravage—I mean live off—a portion of them? How many of your beautiful horses do you have left? To say nothing of your even more beautiful sisters."

"I will get my reward when Prince Cosimo sweeps you from power."

"Bollocks," said Drago crudely, and somebody sniggered. "On both counts."

"Then we must agree," sneered Alessandro, "to disagree."

"On the contrary, Alessandro, I'm afraid your agreement is immaterial here. You are—er—on trial for your life. And whatever nonsense Cosimo has filled your empty head with, I am de facto judge, jury and executioner."

Alessandro's chin lifted even farther, but Esther thought his skin whitened. It came to her that the exaggerated pride of his carriage was merely a cover for the trembling of his limbs. Alessandro was afraid, desperately afraid and determined not to show it.

"I will not crawl to you, Drago. I will not acknowledge your authority in law, whatever powers you hold in fact. I do not even acknowledge you as my equal, since you are base-born."

Beside Esther, Arturo muttered something like, "Imbecile." Drago merely covered another yawn with his long, slender fingers. One of his rings winked in a shaft of sunlight.

Alessandro appeared to be on a roll. "But since you are as near my peer as I can get, I challenge you to try me by combat."

This time, a definite "Ooohhh!" swept around the court

room. Arturo groaned. Esther, her heart beating faster, found herself leaning forward in her seat.

Drago regarded his prisoner with something like amusement. "Really? You expect me to extend your life for a day, while also putting myself to the trouble of extinguishing it myself?"

"You claimed to be judge and executioner," Alessandro sneered.

"So I did."

"So get your own hands dirty for once. Have the courage to let God decide."

A moment longer Drago regarded him, head slightly on one side.

"Aren't you afraid to fight me? With all those legions of hell I have at my beck and call?"

"No," said Alessandro, so defiantly that Esther knew it was a lie. "I have faith in God."

Drago sat back in his chair. "All right," he said casually, as if arranging a game of tennis. "Tomorrow at dawn. Take him away."

"Bloody fool," muttered Arturo. Drago had already risen to his feet, and his clerk, Dandolo, shouted hastily, "Court dismissed."

Drago strode away through the side door, leaving the courtroom in a furious babble of speculation and excitement. Esther turned to Arturo for details, but instead found her arm grasped as he hauled her to her feet and set off with her to the internal door in pursuit of Drago.

ω

The door led into a small antechamber, furnished only with a small round table and two chairs. Drago stood alone by the table, pouring something from a jug into a large silver goblet. He glanced up as they erupted into the room. His lips twisted slightly, he raised the goblet in a toast and drank.

"What the hell did you do that for?" Arturo fumed.

"I was thirsty," said Drago in apparent surprise, lowering the goblet back to the table.

"Stop it," Arturo commanded tightly. "Why did you agree to trial by combat? You can't win, Drago."

He didn't look like a man who couldn't fight. In the book, while preferring less hands-on methods of dealing with his enemies (sorcery and poisoning mainly), he had been both brutal and efficient when cornered. But Esther was learning not to judge anything here by what she had heard of the book. Why could she never get the chance just to *read* it?

"Don't be ridiculous, Arturo," Drago said, refilling the cup, which he waved suddenly at Esther. "*She* could beat him. Hell, even you could, if you practiced."

The shock of his eyes, even glancing off her, left her speechless, although unbidden, a spurt of laughter tried to leap up her throat.

"Then *let* me fight him," Arturo said at once.

"No."

Arturo took a deep breath. "Drago, if he kills you, we're all f...messed," he corrected himself, with a quick, irritable glance at Esther. "And worse, the whole country's stuck with Cosimo. And if *you* kill *him*..."

"Yes, I know, Cosimo says it was by sorcery and my reputation is even blacker. Why does everyone assume I'm an imbecile?"

Without warning, he swung his wild, dark eyes round to Esther, causing her whole stomach to jolt. "What do *you* think?"

She swallowed. "About what?"

"About my imbecility. Do you think I should make judgments based on what my enemies will say about me?"

"Oh no," Esther said with sudden if unspecific anger. "Leave me out if it. I shouldn't even..."

"...be here?" Drago finished for her. "But you *are* here." Deliberately he laid down the cup and strolled round the table to her. "You walked out of Cosimo's camp and straight into my arms. Via a couple of rough soldiers. You *have* to express an opinion."

"I don't *have* to do anything," she said intensely. He stood too close, overwhelming her which made her even angrier. Refusing to be intimidated, she stared back at him defiantly. "And you know damned well you coerced me—somehow—into coming to you. Didn't you?"

He smiled slightly. "Yes."

The blunt confession took her breath away. Panic rose, because it was true—in this world, whatever it was, sorcery existed and he, Drago, was its exponent. It also took the wind out of her sails because she had expected a denial.

As if sensing her reaction, his expression changed quite abruptly. A frown began to form between his arched brows. But Esther didn't want to be an open book to him. Twirling away, she said contemptuously, "For what it's worth, no you shouldn't make judgments based on fear of what your enemies will say. Nor should you make them based on what your *own* people will say. Or on personal whim."

"And which do you imagine I have done?" His voice was

neutral, but she felt his gaze burning into the back of her neck.

"I don't know," she said honestly.

He expelled his breath in a laugh that stirred the tiny hairs on her nape. But her shiver of sensation was lost in the discovery that something in the faint sound was almost...bitter.

Surprised, she turned to face him, but he was already striding out of the room. He didn't look back.

Esther dragged her gaze from the empty doorway to Arturo. "What did I say?" she asked shakily.

Arturo was looking thoughtful. "It's what you didn't say. Or recognize."

"Which is?"

"That his decision was based on the law, as it had to be."

"Then why did he ask me? Why does he care what I say?"

Arturo began to laugh. "I really don't know, but I begin to think it might be amusing to find out."

Chapter Six

Arturo returned her to Drago's quarters after showing her other castle highlights as varied as the banqueting hall and the gleaming new cannons which guarded the fortress and of which he seemed inordinately proud.

"Does Cosimo have cannons?" she asked curiously.

"He did have," Arturo said with such satisfaction that Esther assumed he had been responsible for destroying them. "Though it's not inconceivable he could get more."

"But it wouldn't be easy to take this place, would it?"

"No it wouldn't. But trust me, he'll never get this far."

"How can you know that?" Esther taunted, irritated by his certainty.

Arturo shrugged. "He's been sitting in the same corner of the country for more than a year. If anything, he's losing ground."

"But he's still there."

Arturo sighed. "Yes, he's still there."

Lulled into a sense of friendship, Esther waited for him to enlarge on what he and Drago planned to do about that, but he remained silent as they rounded the corner and into the passage containing Drago's private rooms. With something of a jolt, she realized he didn't trust her.

Marie Treanor

His "friendship" was mere surface courtesy. And what the hell was the matter with her that she wanted anything more from a complete stranger?

I'm alone. That's what's the matter...

Drago's captain took her inside the sitting room, where Lucrezia, almost buried under a pile of mending, beamed at her from a chair under the window. He even kissed her hand gallantly, though spoiled the effect of sophistication by winking at Lucrezia as he departed.

And what the hell does that mean? What does he imagine I am to Drago?

"In you go, madonna," Lucrezia said from her chair, nodding toward the inner door to the bedroom. Her hand flew; the whizzing needle glinted off and on in the sun like a flickering torch. "There's a lovely gown for you on the bed. The prince chose it himself. I'll be in to help you in just a minute."

"Why do I need another gown?" Esther asked vaguely. Already walking to the bedroom door, she was beginning to realize that solitary time might well be a valuable commodity in this strange environment.

"For the banquet," Lucrezia answered, as if she should have known.

Banquet. Now there was to be a banquet. In real life, people paid lots of money to attend medieval banquets. *Real life...?*

Opening the door, she saw him right away. He sat in the window embrasure, his back against the wall, one knee drawn up to his bare chest as he gazed out of the window.

In the fading sunlight, his skin looked golden, stretched across impressively broad shoulders, and the bulging muscles of his arm. He was a perfect physical specimen and just looking at him sent her pulses racing. The urge to touch him was so strong, it almost propelled her across the room.

82

Mind control? Or plain, inconvenient lust?

"Shut the door, Esther." He didn't even turn his head to look at her. With deliberation, Esther lifted her foot and kicked out behind her. The door gave a satisfying slam, but he only acknowledged it with the faintest of smiles.

"What's so fascinating out there?" she enquired.

"Costanzo. I am gloating over my wealth and power."

"Why do you do that?" she asked. It wasn't what she'd meant to say. There had been a crushing retort on the tip of her tongue, but somehow it had got lost and replaced.

At least it made him turn his head lazily and look at her. Then she wished he hadn't, for his eyes were just too—*difficult.*

"Do what?"

"Say outrageous things in that sort of voice, so no one knows if you're joking or not."

Something flickered in his amazing eyes—not quite amusement, not quite bitterness, yet containing something of both. Then his eyelids closed like a hood and when they rose the moment was gone.

He shrugged. "Habit."

For some reason, she had a vision of a proud child, neglected and shamed, alone in a court full of dangerous intrigue. But she didn't want to think of him that way. There was nothing vulnerable about him now, if there ever had been. *She* was the vulnerable one here—which she realized only too well as, with one of his sudden, swift movements, he swung himself off the windowsill and began to walk toward her. He held a shirt, carelessly crumpled in one hand.

Tumbling into speech, because it was easier than letting him advance upon her in silence, she said desperately, "So what were you *really* thinking of as you looked out there?"

He kept coming. She could see every tangled black hair scattered across his chest, leading her eyes inexorably lower to his navel and the beginning of the fine-haired arrow that led down his stomach to....

Christ!

Hastily, she dragged her gaze defiantly back to his.

"Revenge," he said surprisingly. "A dish best served cold, so they say, and I believe I'm shivering. Do you like the dress?"

She backed away from him as he approached, till her heel made contact with the step leading up to the bed and she almost stumbled over. A quick glance showed her a beautiful silk gown of red and gold.

"For tonight," he added before she could speak.

"The banquet," she remembered vaguely.

"Hardly that, but you will dine with me." His hand reached out, touching her hair, and she jerked away as though stung. He followed, hemming her in at the step. She could feel his body heat, smell him, strong and clean and vaguely earthy. She was afraid to breathe in case she touched his naked skin by accident. She wanted to kiss it.

She forced herself to stare directly into his face. Slowly, he lifted the lock of her hair, placing it behind her shoulder. His gaze fell to her neck and his lips curved.

"Soon," he murmured.

"Soon what?" she demanded. Her voice shook slightly, and he must have noticed, for the teasing look came back into his eyes.

"Dinner," he said innocently. He smiled. "I'm hungry, aren't you?"

"No."

He leaned closer till his lips actually brushed her ear,

burning, sending shockwaves of pleasure shooting down her whole body. Her heart was drumming like a rabbit's.

"Liar," he whispered, and something, surely his teeth, grazed her earlobe. She gasped, but already his warmth had gone as he strolled on toward the door.

"Arse-hole," she called after him furiously.

His laughter seemed to surprise both of them, quick and genuine, following him into the outer chamber where he yelled, "Danilo!"

And Esther was left alone at last, trembling like a teenager confronted for the first time by the object of her long-standing crush. How pathetic was that?

ω

Esther's footsteps echoed down the deserted passages which, now that the sun had gone down, seemed both gloomy and threatening. Pale light from the occasional sconce cast more shadow than illumination. Her nerves on edge, her flesh tingling with unspecific fears, she had to force herself to keep walking.

She wondered if there were such things as ghosts in this world. If there were, she was certain they'd haunt this corridor. The ghost of Rudolfo himself, perhaps, or his new wife...

Unsure whether she had been summoned to a banquet or to dine tête-à-tête with the prince, it came as something of a relief to hear the babble and laughter of many voices as she finally swept along the passage toward the open double-doors at the end. This was the banqueting hall Arturo had shown her earlier.

She couldn't see the people inside, but in contrast with the dark, poorly lit passage with its single sconce, the flaring light in the dining room looked blinding.

"My lady." The respectful voice came from her right, from a servant standing beside a smaller door. "This way, if you please."

Esther hesitated, glancing from the servant to the bright light of the dining room. Her heartbeat quickened once more. Private dinner with Drago after all? *Oh Jesus help me...*

The servant said, "This is the way to the prince's own table."

He opened the door beside him and Esther could see that it was at least lit. Shrugging elaborately, she passed the man and went in.

It was a small room, yet another antechamber, containing two cushion-covered benches. A tapestry depicting a banquet scene hung on one wall. On the other a torch flared, casting pale, flickering light over the couple who stood beneath it. Drago, cup in hand, was smiling down into the beautiful face upturned to his.

The woman's arms were wound loosely around his neck. His free hand was raised, almost touching her partially exposed breasts. As if he just had or was just about to caress them.

Esther stopped dead, taken unawares by the strength of the emotions twisting in her gut. A powerful pang of straightforward lust—a desire for it to be *her* semi-naked breast that attracted the prince's caresses. She could almost feel his long, slim fingers there already. Certainly her nipples pressed painfully against the fabric of her gown. She could have dealt with that if it hadn't been for the sheer anger that rose with it, the jealousy that spiked through her like a knife.

In a leisurely sort of a way, Drago looked over the woman's arm at Esther and smiled faintly. He didn't change either his own or the woman's stance. In fact, his finger moved the inch necessary to touch her upper breast—a brief, apparently absent caress that somehow looked quite deliberate. Blood suffused Esther's face. Her whole body burned.

"You're not wearing the gown I picked out for you," Drago observed.

"It made me look like a whore." At least her voice didn't shake. The woman turned at last, regarding her without releasing Drago. Esther ignored her.

"Why should that worry you? Several people have seen you coming out of my bed chamber at various points in the day. Trust me, you already look like a whore."

If there had been anything to hand, Esther would have thrown it at him. Watching her reaction, he smiled cruelly. "Cheer up—there is a certain honour in being my whore. Isn't there?" he added to the woman, just as he broke her hold on him and reached out one peremptory hand to Esther.

"I wouldn't know, would I?" sighed the woman, turning her gaze on Esther at last. Esther merely looked disdainfully at the prince's hand.

"Come," he said impatiently. "Dinner awaits us, and you and I need to talk."

"About what?" Esther snapped.

"Everything. But mainly about you. From your accent, I would guess you are English, like my sister here."

"Your *sister*?" Flabbergasted, Esther glanced from one to the other of them. The woman laughed.

"Stepsister," she said reprovingly, tapping Drago's arm with one plump, dainty finger. Understanding dawned, even before Drago said casually, "Perhaps you already know the lady Matilda?"

Matilda, the heroine of *The Prince of Costanzo*. But that wasn't what kept Esther's stare fixed on her, her feet rooted to the spot. It was the fact that the beautiful lady Matilda wore, quite undoubtedly, the intelligent, secretive face of Margaret Marsden.

ω

In a daze, she found herself escorted into the main dining hall, her hand on Drago's silken arm. How it had got there, she couldn't remember, but for some reason she never even thought of snatching it back. She was seated at the table right beside the tall, throne-like chair that was clearly the prince's—and on her other side sat the living embodiment of Margaret Marsden.

But then was it really so odd? Didn't you always write at least some of yourself into the heroines of your books? Why should Matilda not look like Margaret?

And exactly how insane was she now that she seemed to regard this whole situation as acceptable?

Around her, conversation buzzed as the other dinner guests who had stood for their entrance now re-seated themselves around the various tables that made up the dining hall. Huge tapestries of the same set as the small one in the antechamber decorated the walls here, mirroring the huge mounds of food being placed on the tables, the splashing of wine into goblets, the scuttling of servants and the gluttony of the diners.

"You seem to know me," Matilda said quietly, slipping into the sea beside her. The prince was turned in the other direction, instructing a servant.

"I've seen your portrait," Esther said, watching her with

fascination. She couldn't help thinking that this would give her novel such a boost of realism...to actually *meet* her heroine...!

"Then we never actually met?"

"Hardly," said Esther, on impulse looking her straight in the eyes. She wasn't sure she liked Matilda's eyes. They seemed slyer, less thoughtful than Margaret's. "Apparently you died two hundred years before I was born."

The woman's eyes widened. There was shock there that she couldn't hide, but curiously, no trace of disbelief. Only...avid excitement. Then her lashes came down, veiling her expression and her thoughts.

"Really?" Still, there was excitement behind the drawl. "And yet you recognize me? You must have read my books." A breathless laugh shook her. "But of course you have. *The Prince of Costanzo*, I know it. And yet—two hundred years. How is this possible?"

Good question...

Margaret's smile broadened. Her gaze went beyond Esther, who looked round quickly to see the prince watching them. His face was closed, impenetrable, despite the faint smile that lurked around his mouth. Food was being served onto glittering silver plates.

Only as the servant moved on to Margaret did Drago lean toward Esther.

"So you *do* know each other. From England? Interesting."

"Not *know* exactly." Esther rubbed her forehead in an effort to clear her mind. "I've seen her portrait; I know who she is."

"And her husband, John Fortune. Did you know him in England, too?"

She stared at him. "Is he the key to all this? Christ, you've no idea how weird..." She made a quick movement to stand. "I need to get out of here, I need peace to think ..."

His hand snaked out, pinning her wrist to the table, preventing her from moving.

"No you don't," he said softly. "What you need is to *talk*. To me."

Startled, afraid of the strength in his implacable fingers, she stared up at him. Slowly, the jumble of confused speculation threatening to give her a migraine began to clear away. Stupidly, the only thought she was left with was, *My God, his eyes are beautiful.*

"But first," he warned, "do not trust *her*. Not with anything."

"Ma-Matilda? Why not? Because you've made her jealous of me?"

Disconcertingly, Drago laughed. "She's not jealous of you, strange lady. You dwell on trivia. You must not trust her because she is Fortune's wife."

Esther frowned. "That's another thing. What is she doing here, when Fortune...isn't?"

Drago shrugged. "Apparently, she is trying to negotiate peace between Cosimo and me. In reality, she's spying."

It was said so mater-of-factly that Esther blinked. "You don't seem to mind."

"It's occasionally convenient—not to say amusing—to feed her false information."

"You want me to feed her that tit-bit, too?"

He released her hand at last and lifted his cup instead. "No, I want you to trust me."

For an instant, the surrounding colour and babble faded, forming an imaginary cocoon around her and Drago. His face was very still, his eyes very steady, and she knew a sudden longing to discuss everything with someone, with *him*, to lay this weirdness on his broad shoulders, share it. He might even understand. This strange man who used magic himself would at least be open to possibilities.

But to trust him? The compulsion to tell probably *came* from him, much like her compulsion to leave Cosimo. And while the prince might get away with sorcery, there was no telling what they might do to anyone else practising what they saw as the dark arts. How else would they see her sudden appearance here through the pages of a book?

She blinked, shaking her head blindly. "I can't."

"Because I am insane and evil Drago?"

"Because you are Drago."

His lip quirked. "Don't spare my feelings." Reaching out, he lifted her goblet and pressed it to her fingers. "Drink, eat. And I'll tell you what I think of you."

Absently, she lifted the cup to her lips, tasted the warm, spicy wine flowing over her tongue. Only as her ring winked at her from her finger, was she reminded of the possibilities of poison.

Drago, after all, had poisoned his own father. And Matilda's mother.

She lowered the cup.

He said, "I think you're lost and frightened and need a friend."

Oh Christ, I do...

It came to her from nowhere that it was just as true also of her real life. She was foundering in a relationship that had never worked, in a job that meant nothing to her, dementedly writing second-rate books as a means of escape. Or at least she was very afraid they were second-rate. The novel on Margaret that she had such great hopes of, was just another escape, one that she needed to justify her existence.

Here, in Costanzo, she had nothing and no one. And this man's eyes were too compelling.

Recklessly, she raised her goblet again and drank. After all, he was unlikely to kill her until he had the answers he was looking for.

As another servant piled her plate high with golden chicken wings in a sauce that smelled divine, and a vast array of vegetables, she said, "Perhaps we always need friends. The trick is in choosing the right ones."

His lip curled. "For advancement?"

"That's not a friend, it's a stepping stone."

His eyes gleamed. "For love, then?"

Esther shrugged and took a forkful of chicken. It was tender and delicious and the sauce, creamy and spicy and full of flavours, was to die for. "Got to love your friends." So how had she let all of hers drift away? Because they hadn't got on with Kevin. Like Jenny, her older sister, who no longer spoke to her because they'd quarrelled. About Kevin.

Drago said, "Then I hope to be your friend."

Something in his tone made her a little too warm. Strange flecks of gold flamed in his eyes, fascinating her. The butterflies were back in her stomach, dancing wildly, spreading their heat lower.

And then another figure insinuated itself between them, wearing a dark tunic and hose.

"Forgive the intrusion," said the sardonic voice of Arturo, as he squatted down to their level. "Lady Esther. Sir, a word..." He leaned forward, murmuring something in Drago's ear.

The prince's expression never changed, but he nodded and

rose at once to his feet. "Excuse me," he said casually to Esther and strode off, as if that brief moment of connection had never been.

ω

Away from Drago's distracting presence, Esther could better appreciate the delicacies of the table. Flavoursome, rich and spicy, every dish tempted her to try. She hadn't even been aware how hungry she was.

Arturo, his tongue loosened by wine, sat in the prince's chair and entertained her with stories of Drago's wild past. From dancing across these very tables without once landing in food or drink—a bet accepted by the fifteen-year-old Drago when challenged, it transpired, by the nineteen-year-old Arturo—to more dangerous feats of jumping his horse over peasant huts and riding alone and screaming into a gang of bandits.

"How old was he then?" Esther asked, grateful both for Arturo's loquacity and the fact that he probably wouldn't remember her avid curiosity in the morning.

Arturo frowned. "About the same age," he confessed. He sighed. "It was a difficult time for him. When Prince Rudolfo, his father, named Cosimo and not Drago as his heir."

"He was so desperate to rule, even then?"

"No, no, it wasn't that. It was the kick."

Despite the vagueness of Arturo's answer, Esther glimpsed again the misery of the grief-stricken boy she had dreamed of the first time she'd opened *The Prince of Costanzo*. Was that what had eaten him up? The rejection of his father? Had it also turned him into Margaret Marsden's evil prince?

She said slowly, "And that was why he killed Rudolfo..." She shouldn't even care why, but she did.

Arturo frowned at her. "Do you believe all Cosimo's rubbish? Drago did not kill Rudolfo."

His gaze flickered briefly beyond her shoulder, and she suspected Matilda was listening.

"Then how *did* he die?"

"By poison," Arturo admitted. "But not at Drago's hands."

She had no reason to believe him, no reason to pursue it... "Whose then?" she challenged.

Arturo's smile twisted. He lifted his cup to her as if in a toast. "Guess."

Again his gaze flickered past her, and Esther felt her eyes widen. *Matilda?* Matilda was the true villain here? Margaret herself, along with Fortune and Cosimo? So Drago was the good guy? Did that make any more sense?

"But Drago's illegitimate, isn't he? Whoever killed Rudolfo, he couldn't succeed his father."

"He's perfectly legitimate," Arturo said impatiently. "I told you already. His mother was married to Rudolfo quite legally. The prince discarded her after some indiscretion. She died a few months later, but it was only after Cosimo came to court that Rudolfo began to think of replacing Drago as his heir."

"But that's not..."

"...what Cosimo says?"

She had been about to say "what the book says", but she let it stand.

Arturo helped himself to more fish soup, then waved his hand around the tables. There seemed to be a lot of movement now: many of the jewelled, exotic women were leaving the room.

"Look at this lot. Hard to believe, but this bunch of

reprobates represents the nobility, the old, landed families of Costanzo. Do you really think they would accept an upstart bastard brat as their prince?"

Strong, slender hands gripped the back of Arturo's chair. Drago said amiably, "You forgot evil, insane sorcerer..."

"Usurper and tyrant. I know," Arturo said, standing up without apology. "I was giving her time to get used to the first batch. All well?"

"Fine," the prince replied, sliding like a cat into the vacated chair. He looked directly at Esther. "It was a messenger from my cousin Cosimo. He wants, since I won't negotiate, the lady Matilda returned to him. Along with you."

Esther closed her mouth with a snap. Somehow she had become a pawn between the cousins, which was not a comfortable feeling. Neither was his penetrating gaze, like a cat watching a mouse.

She swallowed. "What did you say?"

"I said I'd think about it and let him know." He reached for the stem of his goblet, playing with it but not lifting it. Unexpectedly, he smiled at her, and her heart lurched.

She said, "I won't be used as a pawn in your games."

"What makes you think you have any choice?" His smile faded, became sardonic. "The fact you can disappear any time you like?"

"It helps." *Although any time I like would help more...*

Between them, forgotten, Arturo stirred. "Any orders?" he asked casually.

"No." The prince glanced at him. It struck Esther at last that the captain was not nearly so drunk as she had imagined. "But feel free to amuse the lady Matilda. Tonight, I have other business on my mind."

As Arturo gave a sardonic nod and made a place for himself on Matilda's other side, Drago's gaze came back to Esther. She returned it with barely understood indignation.

"*Business?*" she repeated, curling her lip.

His dark eyes lit with wicked acknowledgment. The flames began to leap in them again. "Would you rather I'd said 'entertainment'? Or 'desires'?"

She flushed. "No."

"Really? Well if you want the truth I have all three on my mind as I look at you."

Anxiety rose and mixed with excitement and something that came dangerously close to triumph. "Is that meant to flatter me?"

"No. But it's meant to soften you enough that you admit to a little...reciprocation."

Heat swept through her body. It felt like a warning as much as an encouragement. With just a hint of desperation, she said, "Cosimo is right—you *are* insane."

"That may be so...but you can't deny that you want me nonetheless." He leaned forward on the table, his silk-clad arm brushing hers. She could feel his body heat through the thin fabric. She didn't know whether to tear her gaze free of the hypnotic eyes burning into hers or just let herself drown in them.

"In boredom, you can want anything..." *Like Kevin?* The words, tinged with shame, flashed at the back of her mind and were discarded as unimportant in face of Prince Drago's devastating smile.

"But you aren't bored here, are you, strange lady? All this..." He waved his hand around the room. "All this fascinates you. Arturo didn't bore you either. I watched you as I came in.

You're feeling things you're not used to—fear, confusion, outrage, sexual desire. But at least you know you're alive, and you like that. You like it very much."

Another wave of heat swept through her. She wanted to tell him to shut up because he was an asshole. She was terrified someone would interrupt him and he would stop, and the sweet tension building between her legs would fade...

It's his voice, just his voice...and the mind control! Don't forget the mind-control...

His gaze moved to her parted lips. Hastily, she closed them, and he smiled, letting his eyes drop further to the swell of her breasts above the linen gown she had first put on this morning. If she'd worn the other gown, the one he'd sent for the evening, much more of her flesh would have been on show, her breasts pushed together and upward. That would have given him something to look at...

A faint smile lurked around his sensual mouth. His gaze lifted once more to hers. "For example, I bet you're wishing now you'd worn that other gown, so that you could better have displayed your breasts to me."

"You're pathetic," she said shakily. How had he reduced her to this so quickly? He wasn't even touching her save for the casual pressure of his arm, and yet her nipples pushed fiercely at the fabric of her bodice, as if reaching out for his attention. The moisture of desperate arousal soaked between her legs— and since she was wearing no panties it had nowhere to go but to trickle down her inner thighs into the dress.

"Look," he said, flashing his gaze down the table. Following instinctively, Esther saw that while her attention had been so distracted by Arturo and then Drago himself, things had grown much more relaxed. Not to say lax. Wine flowed faster among the remains of the magnificent feast. The noble ladies she had seen earlier had mostly departed and now women of a different character sat in several male laps. One woman had her face buried in her man's neck. Some couples were kissing with abandon. One man, seated beside his woman, bent his head and began to kiss her breasts. His hand came up to cup the covered part and the woman's eyes closed in ecstasy.

Burning, Esther dragged her eyes away, which was a mistake because she immediately encountered Drago's gaze instead.

"I would do that to you," he said. "Now."

A gasp escaped her, of want, of fear that he would, or that he wouldn't, she no longer knew.

"And what's more I think you'd like it. I think you wouldn't care if anyone watched—God's teeth, you might even like that, too. Certainly, you'd invite me closer, draw your gown just a little farther down for me, till your aureoles begin to peep out over the top and my tongue can..."

"Shut up!" she gasped. Furious at the effect of his words on her hot, traitorous body, she scrabbled frantically for defence, and found it in attack. "Do you imagine this will make me reveal the secrets of my sorcery?"

"If it doesn't, it will be such fun trying that I won't care."

She swallowed. She could imagine his hands on her body, his mouth at her breast, tugging sensuously at her nipple. It would feel so wicked, so good...

Furiously, she blinked the vision away. She had to make him stop this. "And if I agree to tell you everything now, will you leave me alone?"

He smiled and reached for his cup. Raising it to his lips he shook his head. "No," he said softly, and drank before lowering the cup. "Face it, Esther. You're captive, and you're mine. You will tell me everything. And I will have you."

If she hadn't been sitting, her legs would have given way.

"Why?" she demanded. "Punishment? Because I doubted your motive for fighting Alessandro de Verini?"

"Maybe," he confessed. "But you won't feel punished."

"I'll feel sick. Why pick on me when you have a court full of whores dying to spread their legs for you? Why pick on the one woman who doesn't want to sleep with you?"

"Because I want her more than them. And because, despite protestations, I'm fairly certain she wants me more than they do. I—er—doubt their motives. Yours is pure lust, and all the more exciting because you're fighting it."

She tried to curl her trembling lips. "Do you imagine you're reading my mind?"

"I've become good at it." He leaned closer, whispered, "Besides, I can smell your arousal."

His finger brushed lightly across the swell of her breast, burning the naked skin, making her gasp. "Why are you *torturing* me?"

He smiled, leaning over her so that she had to bend her head backward to hold his burning gaze. "Because I like it..." The flames seemed to have consumed the darkness of his eyes now. He looked like a devil. His mouth hovered over hers, so close she could almost taste the wine on his breath as it stirred her lips. "Because I can."

"Bastard," she whispered.

"Evil and insane..." His mouth closed over hers, already moving over her lips, opening them wider for his tongue. It was like a sensual tidal wave. She couldn't have fought him if she'd tried. Deliberately, his hand closed over her breast, like a branding before any of his court who cared to look. If there was any doubt before that she was his whore, there would be none now. Even the wild, overtly sensual kiss devastating her mouth was designed to brand her as his, and yet behind it was a curious tenderness she had never expected.

And when he broke it, his eyes blazed into hers with a passion so powerful it terrified her. She had never seen such naked lust in any man's eyes and she was so desperate to taste it she moaned aloud.

"Mine," he whispered, almost in wonder. Then, more harshly, "Mine!"

He sprang to his feet, hauling her with him. "Now."

Chapter Seven

Drago didn't release her until he'd kicked his bed chamber door shut behind the man-servant he'd just unceremoniously ejected. Her heart drummed like thunder in her ears. To maintain her dignity, she thought she should at least object to being dragged out of the suddenly silent dining room in front of his entire court. But before she could do more than open her mouth, he seized her face between his hands and kissed her again.

She hung there, helpless, bombarded by sensation, her breasts heaving with the rhythm of his kiss. Her hands grasped at his arms, his back, fisting convulsively in the silk of his tunic, as if by doing so she could somehow hold on to reality. His mouth grew harder, forcing far more than passive response and, feeling it, he made an inarticulate sound of triumph and pushed his body ruthlessly against her.

For an instant, she felt the hard column of his erection pressing at her stomach before the force of his body made her stumble back against the closed door, but he came with her, slamming his cock against her once more, grinding it into her until she imagined she could feel the very veins of it like ribs. And all the while, his mouth devoured her.

She barely realized that her arms dragged him closer, that her mouth fought back for domination, not just responding but lashing with her tongue, biting, sucking—not until he eventually broke the kiss and grinned at her like a triumphant, reprobate boy.

"Strange lady, I can't breathe. But by the Virgin, you can kiss..."

Esther, blinded by desire, no longer cared about her body's betrayals. She needed him closer, naked, driving that gorgeously huge shaft inside her till she screamed... Reaching up, she tried to take back his mouth, but he only brushed his lips over hers, ran his tongue along her upper lip, with a quick flick under its centre, then moved back out of her arms.

"Deny now that you want me."

She said shakily, "Are you really so insecure that you need to hear it as well as feel it?"

"No. But I like torturing you. And me."

"You?" Her gaze had become rooted on the jutting cock beneath his tunic.

"Trust me, every instant I keep my hands off your delectable body is torturing me."

Without inhibition, he swept his hand over his rigid cock which bulged and pushed at his clothing, and Esther wasn't sure which of them gasped.

He moved away from her, then, to a table under the dark window. A jug and two goblets stood there. Avidly, she watched every movement of his hips and legs as he walked, his quick, strong hands as he splashed dark red wine into the cups.

Only when he turned and commandingly held out a cup to her did she lever herself off the door and walk toward him on legs that trembled.

"So," he said, as she took the wine from him. He let his fingers trail across her knuckles, and she shivered. He smiled slightly. "So, you never met John Fortune before yesterday?"

Esther dragged her eyes free. It felt like a kick in the stomach. She was being seduced for information. Worse, she was too damned hot for even that humiliation to cool her raging desire for him. Was that his sorcery, too?

She said, "You weren't kidding about business, were you?" and was gratified to hear the steadiness of her own casual voice.

"Kidding?" he repeated, puzzled.

"Joking," she translated. "And no, I never met John Fortune before yesterday."

"Well, here's to meeting John Fortune again," he toasted, and raised the wine to his lips. He lowered the cup again, still watching her. "You don't drink?"

"I don't know that I want to meet him again."

"Why not?" he asked, lifting the cup this time to her lips. In surprise, she let the wine splash over them.

"I don't know," she said, when she could speak again. "He seems to be a slightly sinister being..." She broke off with a gasp, for his finger had touched a spot of wine on her mouth and was spreading it lightly along the length of her lower lip.

"Go on."

"I—I think I finished," she said, still against his finger. He leaned over her, and as his finger slid away, he lightly licked over the same path.

"It tastes better on you." Taking her own cup from her suddenly nerveless fingers, he put it back down on the table, and again raised his own goblet to her lips. "Drink," he said, "but don't swallow."

Once again, the heady wine flowed over her lips and into her mouth. But this time, when Drago took the cup away, he replaced it with his lips, brushing, sinking, opening her mouth so that the wine fell into his mouth, too. Through the velvety liquid, his tongue moved into her mouth, savouring the taste, splashing the wine against the back of her teeth. Accepting the strangely sensual game with growing excitement, she let her tongue dance with his, fought with it while the wine flowed back and forth from one mouth to the other, until he sucked it all into his and swallowed.

His mouth left hers, came back, smiling, to brush the last droplet of wine from her lips.

"Then why did you run from me to him?" he said huskily. Esther swallowed. It was so hard to think when her body was on fire, her senses completely absorbed by the strange man seeking information with every caress.

"You sent your soldiers after me. What else was I to do? I just ran. I didn't know Cosimo was there. And before you ask, I'd never met him before yesterday either."

His free hand came up, spanning her throat. "But you think he is the rightful prince."

His long, strong fingers, lightly kneading her throat, could have been a threat. She swallowed, feeling her muscles move under them. As if enchanted, he caressed her skin, following the motion.

Esther said, "He's supposed to be the rightful prince. I don't know anymore."

"Is that why it was so easy to get you to leave him?"

"No, that's because I was bored! And because your— coercion took me by surprise. I won't be so easy to manipulate again."

He smiled. The golden flames leapt in his eyes, scorching her. "You think not? Perhaps we'll experiment with that later on."

His hand slid down the column of her throat, making her shiver, and spread across her shoulder, inched inwards over her chest. Her breath caught as his palm moved over the upper swell of her breast. A fresh flood of moisture began to trickle down her leg. And then his hand fell away.

"So you didn't come to Costanzo looking for him. And you didn't come looking for me." Thoughtfully, his gaze never leaving hers, he dipped one finger into his cup, stirring the wine. "So why did you come to Costanzo?"

"I didn't mean to. I—I don't understand why or how I'm here. I—I thought I was dreaming."

"So where were you?" he asked, removing his finger from the cup and at once tracing a deliberate, thin line of red across the exposed skin of her breasts, his finger rising and falling with the shape of her body. Tiny trickles like red tears began to spill downward from the line. "In the ten years between your appearance in my old bed chamber and yesterday—where did you go?"

All five fingers were in the cup now, and when he withdrew them, he deliberately spattered the wine across her breasts. One spot landed on her chin, several on the bodice of her gown. Instinctively, she wiped at it with her hand, saw his eyes avidly watching her hand draw back and forth across the upper mounds of her breasts. Experimentally, she slid her hand lower, pushed one finger down her cleavage to catch a drip of wine, and heard his breath catch.

New excitement flooded her. Whatever he was doing so deliberately to her, he was definitely not immune to it himself. When she withdrew her hand, he caught it.

She said, "I went back to my real life. In the first instance to the library where I'd fallen asleep over a book. To me, it wasn't ten years. It wasn't even twenty-four hours before I came back."

His eyes never left hers as she spoke, but it was impossible to tell what he was thinking. He seemed more concerned with her hand, lifting it to his lips. His tongue snaked out, winding around the finger she had pushed between her breasts and drawing it into his hot, silken mouth.

Around her finger, he said, "How?" And the vibration of his soft voice spread right up her arm and through the rest of her body, bringing fresh tingles of pleasure.

"I don't know. It's something to do with the book. And maybe because I'm descended from the author..."

Her breath caught. She wondered if she should tell him, what damage it could possibly do. The temptation to confide was strong...and hell, if she could let him play with her body like this, she could tell him everything, see how insane he thought her.

She said, "The author is Margaret Marsden. Who is also Matilda."

His tongue pushed her finger out of his mouth. "Matilda wrote this book?"

"When she was Margaret. Somehow, she ended up in the book, like me. Only the book isn't behaving as it should. The story is different. You're different."

"So...to you, I'm not real? I'm the character in a dream, or a story? Does this feel real?"

Unexpectedly, he tipped the contents of his goblet over her chest. She gasped at the sudden splash of cold on her skin, felt it drain down and into her bodice. The pale linen was stained red as if she'd been shot.

"Quite real," she gasped, instinctively stepping away from him.

"Now you'll have to wear the other gown," he said, apparently pleased. "Tomorrow."

"Now would be good!"

"No," said Drago, placing the empty goblet on the table with a sharp crack. "It wouldn't."

He took her waist in both hands and pulled her back to him. "I'll take care of it for you." His head bent. She felt his mouth roving across the skin of her chest, his lips, his tongue soaking up the spilled wine, drifting lower to the neck of her gown.

Esther couldn't breathe. His mouth scorched her, not just where it touched, but somehow all over her trembling body. His beard grazed her breast. His tongue slipped down her cleavage, as once her finger had to tease him, probed beneath the neckline of her gown, pushing it downward to let him at the wine underneath. His teeth dragged it lower still. He lifted his head slightly.

"Now I see your aureoles," he whispered. "Dark, and stained with wine..."

They were. Only just hidden by the fabric, her nipples stood out painfully, begging for attention that she was desperately sure they would get. His tongue snaked out, teasing first one dark, puckered aureole, then the other. His lips brushed them, making her ache with pleasure.

Helplessly, her arms rose to hold him, then fearfully fell back to her sides. She didn't know if she was afraid to encourage him or afraid that he would stop if she distracted him at all.

His tongue pushed beneath the neckline, captured a nipple and drew it free. Esther gasped as sensation washed over her. He paused to look at her other breast, watched as her panting breath gradually released the nipple from the fabric. He smiled,

107

and slowly took the first nipple into his mouth.

Esther moaned. Without thought now, she closed both arms around him, spread her palms across the heat of his back. The silk felt damp with his sweat. Tenderly, he brushed his mouth back and forward across her nipple, flickering his tongue across it, too. Shocks of delight swept through her, and when his hand came up to cup the underside of her other breast, caressing higher, his thumb brushing the aching peak of her nipple just as his tongue did with the other, she thought she would die of pleasure. The aching fire in her loins was so urgent, she thought she would come just from his touch on her breast.

"Do you like that, Esther?" he whispered around her nipple, sending fresh sensation scattering through her. "Surely this is the best pleasure-dream you ever had...better than reading forbidden books for titillation..."

She gasped as he flicked her nipple strongly with his tongue and released her breast. With one tug, both gown and undergown dropped to her elbows, revealing most of her upper body. Sweeping his hands up her arms, he pulled the clothing free till it fell around her ankles and his gaze raked her from head to toe.

She burned, with desire, with need, with embarrassment and fear that he wouldn't like what he saw. Kevin didn't seem to, not anymore, if he had ever been very interested in her body.... She had put on weight, of course, though surely...

"Nothing else matters" he whispered. "You are mine. And so beautiful I could weep."

He didn't weep. Still in shock, she felt his arms go around her, lift her against his hard, hot body and surely he, too, was trembling? His cock pressed into her abdomen, so much more distinct and powerful without her gown in the way. She wanted desperately to feel it driving inside her. Standing on tip toe she wriggled until it fit in the hot, tender place between her legs, and moaned.

She reached up for his mouth, found it slammed into hers in a kiss so ferocious she thought it would tear her apart. And yet everything in her leapt toward him. She gloried in his fierce passion, matched it.

The world swayed as he swept her up in his arms, strode across the room and up the three steps to his bed, where he laid her among the luxurious pillows. For one glorious moment, he lay with her, his weight stretched out on top of her so that she felt every clothed inch of him on her naked body, the heat of his hard cock pressing between her legs. Her pussy throbbed for him.

And then, releasing her mouth, he shifted his body to lie beside her. She opened her eyes to find his blazing with pure, powerful lust, and she couldn't prevent her moan of need, of anticipation.

He smiled wolfishly, deliberately slowing his panting breath.

"Now we'll see," he said huskily. "How much can you resist me?"

He moved over her again, catching her hands and raising them high above her head on the pillows. His eyes stared into hers for a long moment.

"You mustn't move your hands. They are bound."

He released them and as he slipped down the bed, his hands caressing her legs from thigh to knee, making her gasp, she tried to reach out to hold him, touch him. Her arms wouldn't move.

"Drago!" she whispered in sudden fear.

He laughed softly and kissed the side of her knee. "I'll release you," he promised. "In time. Enjoy it. Christ knows I will."

She cried out with surprise as he pushed her legs wide and held them apart for his avid view. Gradually, as his hot gaze moved across her body, from her soaking pussy and her thighs to her stomach and breasts, the fear and the embarrassment began to fade into something approaching wonder.

He wasn't just tolerating what he saw. He *liked* it. He *wanted* her, and with an urgency she had never seen in another man.

"Naked and open to me," he whispered. "Glistening like rose petals in the rain... I can take you now, like this, without even undressing." His hands went to his cock, delving under his tunic, wrenching at the fastenings. "I can push my cock straight into you, you're so wet for me already, and I can fuck you till we both scream the castle down. Would you like that, strange lady?"

Neither arms nor legs would obey her and move. But at his words, her hips lifted off the bed, arching, pleading. No one had ever spoken to her like this and it drove her to insanity.

"Yes," she gasped. "Yes, I'd like that!"

His lips quirked again. "Good."

He freed his cock, which stood out huge and dark against the whiteness of his hand, mesmerizing her. She swallowed, and wriggled, bucking under his gaze. His smile widened. His hand swept over the weeping head of his cock. His other hand reached between her legs, cupping her pussy, and pressed.

Somewhere, the aching tension broke. She cried out as the waves of orgasm began to roll.

He muttered something unintelligible, and without removing his hand, fell on her body, crushing her mouth under his, holding and kneading her breast as the ecstasy tore her apart, convulsing her body beneath him. She had never known anything like it. It was like a hurricane sweeping through her body, howling pleasure that never ended in gust after gust. His hand on her pussy began to move, exploring and stirring, holding her there as his fingers glided across the swollen nub of her clitoris, sparking new bliss from the spent.

She ached to hold him, and yet the very helplessness of her position brought its own, novel pleasure. She let herself drown in his mouth, in his hands, in the blinding, all-encompassing joy.

When at last it began to die away, he released her mouth and she became aware of his eyes blazing black and yellow with lust.

"So you can know pleasure," he almost purred. "I like that. Can you give it, too?"

"Let me try," she whispered breathlessly, smiling through her tangled hair. Her sated body tingled still, began to reignite as, kneeling between her legs, he tore off his tunic and shirt and hose. The latent strength in his broad chest and shoulders fascinated her. Muscles bulged in his upper arms, particularly his right. His sword arm. His cock stood up rigidly to attention.

He straddled her. She moaned aloud with fresh, urgent anticipation. With a strange, spiralling feeling, she felt the invisible bonds unwind. Joyfully, she stretched up both arms for him, inviting him closer, inviting him into her welcoming body.

And yet before she could touch him, something dragged her arms back. They fell to her sides. Impossible weights pinned her to the bed. The world began to move and sway.

"No!" she cried out in fury. "Not now, not now!"

But there was nothing she could do, except watch Drago's

suddenly concerned face swing into darkness and disappear.

Chapter Eight

"Esther! *Esther!*"

Her face was stinging. It was Kevin's voice dragging her back, his hand slapping at her cheek. She was slumped in the chair by the desk, in the Hays' library. Her host stood behind Kevin, gazing down at her with concern but just a little more excitement than Kevin. He held *The Prince of Costanzo* open in his hands.

It's touching the book that does it. When I stop touching it, if I drop it or if they take it from me, then I come back. But he's touching it now and he's still here. I'm right, it must be because I'm related to Margaret... How the hell did she do that? Using Fortune's book?

"Stop it," she mumbled irritably, struggling to sit up as Kevin slapped her again. "Kevin, *stop it!* I'm awake!"

"Thank Christ for that! We were beginning to think you were dead."

"Don't be daft."

"Not so daft as you might think," Hay said thoughtfully. His thumb caressed the page of *The Prince* and she watched it, entranced.

If I did that, I'd be back there. He'd be making love to me. Oh Jesus...

Her body was still on fire. The memory of his hands and his lips on her was palpable, and the after-glow of orgasm mingled most distractingly with unsatisfied lust. Her pussy felt wet and sticky. She could still feel the weight of his body, the touch of his fingers, like an echo.

She swallowed, trying to keep her mind on the present. At least she was wearing her own clothes and her shakiness could easily be put down to disorientation.

Hay was saying, "You were very deeply asleep you know. We could barely find a pulse."

My pulses were all in Costanzo, beating for him, *for Drago...*

"It was almost like..." Hay broke off, but he already had Esther's attention.

She stared at him. "Like catalepsy?"

"Or whatever it was that Margaret Marsden appeared to suffer from."

"Well that makes sense!" Esther said excitedly. Margaret had fallen into the book, too, only somehow had managed to stay there, was *still* there nearly two hundred years later. While her body remained at home, finally so catatonic that her embarrassed family gave out she had disappeared. They must have suspected magic, and that was why they wanted no one to see her. Yes, it began to make perfect sense...

"Not to me, it doesn't," said Hay, looking at her closely.

Kevin said, "Are you all right now? Because I think it's time we were going."

Esther jumped up with quick guilt. How long had she been asleep? Longer, she suspected, than the half-hour Hay had originally given her to study Fortune's book—which she hadn't even looked at.

But then, why had he suggested she do that? To see what

happened to her when she read *The Prince of Costanzo*? He already suspected something to do with the book, only whatever it was never happened to him...

Distracted by speculation, she was already at the door with Kevin before the idea hit her. Impulsively, she turned to see Hay slowly laying *The Prince* back down on the desk she regarded as hers.

"Sir Ian?"

He glanced up.

She took a deep breath. "I won't sell your wife my ring. But I would swap it for the book, for *The Prince of Costanzo*."

Hay's thin lips closed. His face gave little away, even when he smiled.

"My dear, that wouldn't please either of us."

ω

"What did he mean by that?" Esther wondered. They were back in their room above the pub, from where the rumble of conversation mingled with the occasional burst of raucous laughter.

Kevin, emerging from the bathroom in his grey sleeping shorts and top, didn't look very interested.

"By what?"

"That it wouldn't please either of us to swap the book for the ring."

"Because we wouldn't get the twenty thousand from Lady Hay, and he'd lose his precious book. Just sell it to her, Esther. You know, I think he liked me. I think he was sizing me up for a senior position in his organization."

"Would you want to move at this stage?"

Kevin shrugged irritably. "I might. If it was the right job."

"Mmm." She gazed at the ring on her finger. Half of her was relieved that Hay had rejected her impulsive offer. She really didn't want to lose the ring. It was like part of herself, her link with the past. With Margaret, who was not quite as she'd imagined her...

And yet after tomorrow, she would be denied access to the book. She wouldn't be able to get back to Costanzo, to Drago...

Butterflies fluttered in her stomach. Her whole body felt warm with memory, with desire and with something less tangible, something curiously gentle yet intense. Like something coming alive in her.

Her breath caught.

How had Margaret managed to stay? Was she, Esther, seriously considering giving up her world, her life, for an imaginary one? Would her body here just slip into a coma and die?

Could she really give herself to the unpredictable Drago? The man was blatantly seducing her for information, and she loved it. Which was pathetic enough, but when he dumped her, how would she feel then? He never even pretended to care for her, though the lust was real enough...

Was he like that with every woman who attracted his erratic attention? She didn't know. The truth was, she knew nothing about him, and all the contradictory glimpses had achieved was to fascinate her, making her more and more curious to know the man and what made him tick.

Because somehow it wasn't Margaret who made him tick. Though she had never managed to read *The Prince of Costanzo*, not even the smallest description of Drago, she had read the few contemporary reviews that had made publication before the

116

book had been withdrawn, as well as more modern analyses of these. And Drago, her Drago, was nothing like Margaret's Gothic villain.

Well, he might be a villain. The jury was still out on that one, despite Arturo's eloquent defence. He was accused of killing his father and his stepmother, of illegally usurping his cousin's throne. He admitted to being a sorcerer, as Margaret had written him, and he was certainly handsome and clever and charming. But where was the insane cruelty, the tyranny? In the court, he had shown only justice. Arturo, the people of the court showed him respect and even liking—*love?* And she was sure that wasn't induced by fear, or even magic. It was like...Drago was his own man...

What if he was? What if they all were? What if that world, Costanzo, had *always* existed? What if Margaret had discovered it, written about it in a manner acceptable to her audience, and then, unable to stay away, had simply jumped in for good?

"Come to bed, Esther and put the light out," Kevin said impatiently.

Startled, Esther stared at him. He closed his eyed pointedly and pulled the quilt up to his ears.

It was stupid. Maybe she knew nothing about Drago. Drago may not even be real outside her own diseased mind. And yet suddenly he seemed more solid, more known than the man with whom she was about to share a bed. The stranger she was going to marry.

She licked her dry lips. An hour ago she had lain trembling in Drago's arms, convulsed by orgasm before he'd even entered her body. She'd never even *thought* of Kevin then. What sort of a slut was she?

She could jump Kevin now, try to assuage her raging lust for another man with her fiancé.

No she couldn't.

Abruptly, she turned away and lifted the lid on her laptop.

"I won't be long," she said. "I just want to check something first."

Was there to be a lifetime of those peevish sighs and angry huffs? She wouldn't mind them, if only they ever laughed, if they ever even had a conversation worth a damn, but she couldn't even remember the last time that had happened.

What the hell am I doing here?

ω

Two hours later, she closed the laptop with a snap, considerably the wiser about the studies of John Fortune, who had travelled all over Europe, Russia, Asia and Africa learning his arts. And, strangely, quite certain about what to do with her real life.

It was time. Way past time.

She gazed across to the bed. In the pale glow of the lamp, all she could see was a flop of brown hair, and the profile of his jaw and cheek. It was so familiar it made her heart ache. For a loss already passed.

"Kevin? Kevin, are you awake?"

"I am now!"

Ignoring that, she said urgently, "Kevin, can you even remember why we're together?"

He didn't even open his eyes. "Of course I can. We're getting married."

"No we're not. For some reason, we *engaged* to get married, and I can't even remember why we did that now. You know what I think? I think we'd just been together so long, we expected our relationship to be at another level. It was, but we didn't see it. We tried to force it to the next stage by 'getting engaged' like everyone else. When what we should have been doing was ending it."

He did open his eyes at that. Staring at her, he said, "We'll talk about it tomorrow. Just get some sleep, will you?"

"No. I can't sleep. Look, we found each other several years ago when we were both at a low, and then we couldn't find a reason to part. Well, I've found that reason."

Slowly, he sat up. "What exactly are you saying?"

Esther smiled, sadly. "That we shouldn't be together. We're wasting each other's lives. Let's finish it now."

"Now?" he said, bewildered. "Right now?"

"Right now."

"But what about Steve's wedding?"

She almost laughed. Part of her wanted to cry. "It'll still happen without me. And your mates can all console you by telling you what a bitch I am. Or *you* can tell them what a bitch I am, and that's why you dumped me."

She was fairly sure the latter is what he would tell them anyway.

ω

Kevin didn't drive far. He knew she was awake when he left the room, took what satisfaction he could from leaving her without a word. After three years. Pride and anger carried him to the car, got him inside and out of the pub car park. He knew she was watching him from the window, for some sign of farewell, but he was damned if he would give it to her.

Who the hell did she think she was? How could she *do* this?

He'd driven out of the village, beyond the drive leading up to the Hays' mansion before it came to him that he'd no idea where he was going or why. Pulling up by the side of the road, he stared bleakly at two cows. They regarded him incuriously as they continued to ruminate.

Kevin was not normally an indecisive man. How could she have reduced him to this?

Because for the first time in three years, she's taken you by surprise.

To hell with her!

Decisively, he took his mobile from his inside pocket and dialled Steve. After a couple of rings, his friend's voice came over sleepily. "Kevin? What the fuck are you doing up at this time?"

"Don't know, to be honest." Kevin sighed. "It seemed the right thing to do."

There was a pause, then Steve said, "What's the matter?"

"Esther."

"She keeping you at that village for another day?" The grin was back in Steve's voice, making him wince. Steve and the lads didn't think much of him for giving into Esther's wish to spend several days in this God-forsaken dump. "You *are* going to make it to the wedding? I'm counting on you, mate."

"I'll make it to the wedding. Esther won't."

There was another pause. "Ah. You've had a tiff."

"Rather more than that, actually. She—dumped me. Right out of the blue."

"*She* dumped *you?*"

Just for an instant, he wished he'd told the lie he would tell everyone else, that he had dumped her. But he realized that he was looking to Steve for advice. Steve was one step ahead of him, getting married tomorrow.

"Yes, amazing, isn't it?" Kevin mourned.

"What the hell for? You haven't been playing away from home, have you, Kev?"

"No no, it's nothing like that. She just woke me up last night to tell me it was over."

"But she must have said *why*."

"Something to do with us never getting around to the marriage thing, and never reaching the right level of our relationship, or some such girl-shit."

"Ah, well, you should have set a date by now Kevin-boy. The girl's feeling un-loved. Like your mum's cat, you've got to pet it once in a while."

"Well it's too late now for such sound advice."

"Nonsense! Trust me, the worst thing you can do is leave now. You need to make a stand, mate, show her who's boss. She doesn't want you to leave. She just wants you to pay a little attention to her. So go dig her out of that damned library now and bring her down here. Sarah will talk some sense to her while you and I head pubward with the lads."

This sounded such an attractive solution that in spite of his rather severe doubts, Kevin found himself saying, "You really think she didn't mean it?"

"Of course not. She wants a reaction, that's all."

"I'm not sure you're right there, Steve. To be honest, she seems rather more interested in her stupid research than me. She wouldn't even sell that bloody awful ring she likes so much, when she was offered a fucking good price for it. Nearly twenty grand!"

"*Twenty grand?*" Steve exclaimed. His voice faded as if he was staring at the phone for confirmation. "Are you sure? And Esther turned it down? *Why*, for God's sake?"

"No reason at all. She says it's a family heirloom. It's certainly hideous enough."

"Well, this does rather change things," Steve mused. "Or does it?"

Silence filled the phone. "Steve? Are you still there?"

"Yes, of course I am. Listen, I'm going to drive up there now. We'll go and get Esther back, and get you the money for the ring—just the thing to set you up. And tonight the drinks are on you. Now, where exactly are you?"

ω

Behind the inevitable sorrow of a broken relationship, excitement fought its way up. Freedom from Kevin was exhilarating, and as she walked up the long drive to the Hays' house—Kevin had taken the car—she began to make vague plans.

Suddenly, she was very aware of her own strength, of her legs striding out, arms swinging by her sides, her heart beating steadily with excitement, with sheer joy in life, her lungs drawing in the fresh, sweet-smelling air of the countryside after rain. She could do anything, anything at all.

She could resign from the dull job. For a few months, she could live off the money she'd saved for the wedding, while she wrote the book about Margaret.

But that was her future life. Today, she could go back to Costanzo. To Drago...

Excitement burned. She didn't care if she was insane. Or if *he* was. A few stolen hours in his company was worth more, made her more alive than any amount of time spent with anyone else *ever* had.

It was the aloof housekeeper who opened the door and showed her to the library. The rest of the house seemed quiet as the grave. Esther hoped it had been a good party.

The Prince of Costanzo caught her eye as soon as she went in. Relief flooded her, for she'd lived in terror of Hay removing the book after she'd betrayed her desire to own it. But it lay on the table where he'd left it last night, looking ordinary and a little dusty. And yet she could feel the pull of it from the door. It was like Drago's compulsion, when he had made her leave Cosimo's camp, only this time, she knew a large part of the compulsion came from herself. She was desperate just to grab the book and delve straight in.

Who knew? Drago might still be making love to her. What happened to her body in Costanzo when she was here...?

Determinedly disciplined, she laid down her jacket, sat at the desk and picked up John Fortune's book on necromancy. A quick scan bore out much of what she had read on the Internet last night, but even more interesting, another phrase caught her eye: "magikal objects as a gateway to captured souls".

Reading around the line, she couldn't make much sense of it. He merely listed it as something he had discovered in his travels, but unlike most of his list, he never expanded on it.

Esther frowned. Is that what *The Prince* was? A gateway to other souls? And yet the book had been written two hundred years after Fortune's death! She had never heard that Margaret dabbled in magic...although of course there was all the supernatural stuff in her stories. Perhaps that was more than imagination.

And what did "captured" mean?

Thoughtfully, she closed the book and laid it down. As she did so, her ring winked under the electric light and she paused, staring at it.

"My dear, that wouldn't please either of us."

Hay knew. There was no point in swapping the book and the ring. You needed both to get into Costanzo.

Esther tugged the ring off her finger and laid it down on the desk. Then she reached for *The Prince* and opened it at random.

"The castle was in darkness and Matilda imagined she could hear the whispering of souls among the soft footsteps which echoed in the dank passage."

No swirling, no swaying world, nothing to drag her in.

Apart from "Chapter One", those were the first words in the book she had actually read.

She remembered something else—John Fortune's recognition of the ring. Had it been his? Had he somehow given it to Margaret through Matilda? Jesus, which of them had come first, Margaret or Matilda? Was the woman she had met so briefly a combination of souls? Was Drago? Hell, was she, Esther, when she went there, somehow bound with another soul? She still *felt* like Esther...

Reaching for the ring, Esther slid it back on to her finger. Somewhere among these letters, she was sure she would find a reference to a ring, perhaps acquired from an unlikely source, without Lord Hawton's knowledge perhaps. She would check it out later. For now, she couldn't fight it any longer.

She picked up *The Prince of Costanzo* again let the pages fall open where they would, and deliberately placed her right hand over them. The ring winked at her as the print spun and drew her in.

Chapter Nine

She lay naked in Drago's bed in the pale grey light of dawn. For a moment, she didn't move, simply listened for the sound of his breathing, tried to feel the heat of his body, the excitement he always brought with him.

She was alone. Disappointment swept over her like a wave. Stupid to think she could pick up exactly where she left off. The last time she came back, several hours had passed. Perhaps it was the same again.

Surely it wouldn't be ten years like the first time?

As she rose from the big bed, she saw the imprint of his head on the pillow, of his body on the mattress where the covers had been pulled back. When she touched it, she imagined it was still warm. Relief flooded her. He hadn't been gone long.

Prowling around the room, she could find no clothes, not the wine-stained gown she'd worn yesterday, nor the lower-cut one he'd expected her to wear in the evening.

The chests and cupboards were full of his clothes, shirts, tunics, cloaks.

In desperation, she dragged the sheet around her and went to the door.

In the centre of the outer room, two people who had been

squaring up to each other turned their heads and gaped at her open-mouthed. Lucrezia and the man-servant whom Drago had thrown out of the bed chamber last night. If it was last night.

"Um—where are my clothes?"

Lucrezia bustled forward. "I have something nice for you here. In you go!"

"Where is Drago?" Esther asked as soon as Lucrezia came in bearing silken garments.

"Fighting." Lucrezia pursed her lips with disapproval. Esther stared at her uncomprehendingly before she remembered.

"Alessandro! Now?"

"Unless he's already finished it."

Esther felt her face whiten. "Who's finished it? Who do you expect to win?"

"The prince, of course."

She hadn't really doubted it. She swallowed, and let Lucrezia drop the underdress over her head. "Will he kill Alessandro?"

"What do you think?" Lucrezia said tersely. Esther gave her another look.

"You don't approve," she observed.

"I don't approve of a lot that goes on around here, but it's hardly my place to change things. Left to themselves, men will always settle things by fighting and killing. Where God comes into it is beyond me."

"And me," said Esther ruefully. Lucrezia glanced at her, and moved to fasten the overdress. It was amber silk, slashed to reveal the darker fabric beneath. A band of elegant gold embroidery across her breasts divided the gown from the higher necked underdress that protected her modesty. Such as it was.

"Well perhaps *you* will have some influence with him. Oh it's too late for Alessandro de Verini, and let's face it, the man's a traitor, but for others... Perhaps you can help end this stupid war, make peace between the prince and his cousin. She—the lady Matilda—is supposed to be doing that, but it seems to me all she's interested in is trying to commit mortal sin with her stepbrother."

"Which mortal sin?" Esther asked, thinking of poison and stilettos.

"Fornication," said Lucrezia darkly. "Adultery. With her brother!"

"He's not her brother," Esther protested. "There is no blood relationship at all." And why the hell was she defending what made her feel sick? She saw again the vision of them before dinner last night...

"There is to God," Lucrezia insisted. "But he has *you* now...doesn't he?"

Unexpectedly, the woman's eyes bored into hers. Esther stared back at her, seeing the fierce protection of a mother wolf, the stern discipline of a school teacher.

She said low, "I don't know. I shouldn't even be here..."

"I told him that." Lucrezia nodded. "'That's no way to treat a gentle lady,' I told him, but he goes his own way. Take my advice and deny him—it's the only lever we women have sometimes."

With Lucrezia's words ringing in her numb ears, Esther fled, only realizing when she was in the passage that she hadn't asked where the "trial by combat" was taking place.

In the end, she found it easily by following the noise. The big front doors of the castle stood open, and the guards and doormen seemed to have formed a relay system by which those nearest the action passed on the news to their comrades, all the way down the line as far as the kitchens.

"Alessandro's on his knees!"

"The prince has him!"

"Bugger, he's let him up again..."

"Alessandro's bouncing back! He's got new energy from somewhere, for he's pressing hard now!"

Esther hurried along, her heart drumming in her ears. She didn't know if she feared more for Drago or for what he might do to Alessandro. She didn't want to see it, for she knew it would be nothing like cinema swashbuckling. This would be a real battle, with blood and brutality and crunching bones and spilling gore, and the whole idea made her nauseous. Yet she couldn't stay away.

When she found the central courtyard where it was all happening, people recognized her and let her through to the front of the crowd. Because they thought she was the prince's mistress? *Was* she? Which act changed you from a flirt to a mistress? Orgasming under his hard, tender hand? The memory brought a rush of unexpected and unwelcome heat, a longing to repeat it and much, much more.

They fought without armour. Alessandro, panting, his hair plastered onto his skull, wore his tunic, now cut and stained with sweat and blood. He stood bent in the middle of the courtyard, his sword held desperately in front of him like a shield, a wicked dagger grasped in his other hand which hung almost limply to the side, simply defending himself against Drago's onslaught. He looked like a man in hell.

Drago, on the other hand, was having a whale of a time. The joy of battle made his eyes glow. Wearing only shirt and leggings, he hacked and slashed with abandon, using both sword and dagger to drive Alessandro back and back.

Giving ground constantly, Alessandro made the occasional

lunge, as if desperately hoping for a lucky strike. Drago always deflected it, almost casually. Esther had the impression this had been going on for a long time. Both men were tired, but only a miracle could save Alessandro now.

Am I that miracle? Am I supposed to step in and save Alessandro's life? Would Drago listen to me, or just kill me, too?

She didn't believe he would do that.

Alessandro's arm shook with the effort of maintaining his grip on his sword as Drago pushed his own up to disarm him. From somewhere, Alessandro gave a massive heave, pushing Drago off a little way, and lunged after him. Drago parried. At the same time Drago's foot shot out, hooking Alessandro's legs from under him, and as the defendant fell, his sword flew across the yard.

Drago was on him already, his knee in Alessandro's chest, his sword at his throat.

The babble of excitement in the yard broke off. In eerie silence, everyone looked on, as paralyzed as Esther by the speed of the end, by the solemnity of the moment. A life about to end.

Impulsively, she pushed forward. A hand caught her arm. Arturo, shaking his head at her, his finger to his lips. Uncomprehending, she stared at him.

From several feet away, Alessandro was speaking, his voice agonized and breathless.

"I've lost. Is God really on your side? Or is it the Devil after all?"

"Who knows?" Drago sounded almost conversational. His voice barely wavered, his hand was steady as a rock as it held the sword point to his enemy's jugular. "It might be heresy, of course, but my personal belief is that neither of them gives a shit about trivia like this."

"Trivia?" Alessandro was outraged.

"In the grand scheme of the world," Drago explained apologetically. "I don't suppose your betrayal matters much to anyone but you and me. And Cosimo, who will have to go after your heir now instead. And your people, of course, who will continue to be exploited by my cousin, forced to fight in his army, feed his mercenaries, die of hunger or brutality or battle while their once-prosperous land dies around them, too."

"You are describing your own regime!" Alessandro cried. His aim seemed to be for contempt, but he sounded more despairing.

"Oh no," said Drago. "Don't you remember how it was before Cosimo came back? Compare the west then and now. And didn't you notice the land *here*, Alessandro? It thrives. No one dies of hunger. My soldiers are properly housed and disciplined. No one lives in fear."

"I saw nothing!" Alessandro panted.

Drago lifted his sword and replaced it negligently in his scabbard. "Come, I'll show you."

He stretched down his hand to Alessandro who stared at it, then lifted his eyes to Drago.

He said, "You really are insane, aren't you? Are you going to kill me later instead? Have your executioner do it?"

"Guess," Drago said brightly. His hand didn't waver. Still, nobody spoke or moved. Eventually, Alessandro reached up, gingerly taking the outstretched hand, and Drago hauled him to his feet.

"Horses!" called the prince.

"Now?" Alessandro demanded, still bewildered. Seconds ago, he'd awaited imminent death by the judgment of God and the hand of the prince. Now he faced some sort of reprieve by his enemy.

"Now," said Drago as two grooms ran into the courtyard with bridled and saddled horses clopping beside them. "Do you need a leg up like a girl, or can you manage?"

A strange sound came from Alessandro's throat. It sounded like laughter.

Esther slowly turned to look at Arturo. The soldier grinned at her and winked, then pushed away through the crowd and disappeared.

The fighters, mounted, rode at a trot to the gate. Drago looked unconcerned, as if he knew his prisoner wouldn't even try to escape. Esther thought he was right. Alessandro was too bewildered, too curious.

Lucrezia was wrong, she realized. Drago was changing things himself. He didn't need her.

She continued to stand there while the crowd of watchers dispersed around her, arguing or laughing over what they had just seen, admiring the fight, debating the rights and wrongs of the prince's mercy, laying bets on whose side Alessandro would choose by dinner time.

They were in awe of their prince. He was odd, he was unpredictable and often incomprehensible, but they had a definite pride in him. Not Margaret's Drago at all, who ruled by ruthless cruelty and fear.

Distractedly, she brought up her left hand to play with the ring on her right. It was an old, nervous habit, and she rarely realized she was doing it. On this occasion she noticed because there was nothing to play with. Her finger was bare. The ring was gone.

ω

After dementedly searching Drago's room and questioning both Lucrezia and Drago's body servant, who was called Danilo, Esther found another servant to take her to Matilda.

Margaret Marsden sat in the arched courtyard she could see from Drago's chamber. Although the women of the court appeared to be giving her a wide berth, she had no shortage of male admirers, clustered around her like moths to a flame while others cast her side-long looks as they strolled past with their own less attractive partners.

Esther suspected she had done Matilda-Margaret this favour—if such it was—by distracting the prince from her and so making Matilda fair game to the rest of the male court.

With something of an unwelcome jolt, she realized Drago was treating her as he had formerly treated Matilda, flirting, seeking advantage and information through seduction. Had his eyes really looked at his stepsister with the same flaring lust? Had he touched her with the same tenderness, making her believe that his desire at least was genuine and something just a little more than a passing grope? Was that, too, part of Drago's talent? Playing everyone?

And what the hell did it matter anyway? She needed her ring and she needed to get back to the real world and write a book. She needed to *live*.

The servant insinuated himself into Matilda's little court, murmuring to her, politely indicating Esther's presence.

Matilda glanced up and smiled graciously at her over the servant's shoulder. When he effaced himself, she stood at once, and the men fell back like crumbs shaken from a cake.

"Esther. I've been hoping for a chat with you."

"Likewise," Esther said intensely. "I need to know what's happening, how this place exists, how you and I are here. How you can *still* be here! And more stuff I haven't even thought of yet. But first..."

"Why?" Matilda-Margaret interrupted. "Because knowledge is power?"

Esther stared at her. The writer's green eyes were mocking, superior, filled with an understanding that made Esther want to slap her.

"What sort of power could I possibly have—or want—in a place that doesn't exist outside of *your* imagination?"

Margaret laughed, a pretty, tinkling sound that grated on Esther's nerves. She took her arm, urging her to walk with her, and under the pretext of patting her hand, actually pinched her skin painfully.

Esther jerked her hand free. "What the...?"

"That was real enough, wasn't it? Not my imagination, but your sensation. You really have no idea about this place."

"I thought I just said that."

Margaret smiled. "So you did. So what can I tell you?"

"Where my ring is, to start with."

"What ring?" She sounded bored.

"The one you saw on my right hand last night."

"Oh, you mean *my* ring."

Esther looked at her. There was contempt in that admission. A belief that she could do exactly as she liked.

"No, the one you passed on to your daughter when you died. The one which is now mine."

Margaret smiled lazily. "Do I look dead to you?"

"Do I look stupid to you?"

"From here? Oh yes."

"Look, you want me out of your hair, give me the ring so I

133

can get back!"

"My dear, you don't need the ring to get back. Sooner or later, someone will take the book from you, and you'll be back home. Wherever that is."

"But I won't be able to get back *here...*"

Margaret smiled. "Oh dear."

Esther's breath caught. So that was it. Margaret—Matilda, whoever she was—wanted her gone. Because she upset her plans? Because of Drago...? Well that was stupid, for Esther was pretty certain that neither of them made much difference to Drago.

"So how come *you* never went home? How could you stay here all those years without the ring?"

"Because I'm part of this world now. Seriously, you should leave—and stay away—before you become part of it, too. For after that, there will be no getting home."

Margaret lifted the little fan in her right hand and lightly patted Esther's numb cheek with it. "That frightens you, doesn't it?" she said indulgently. "Go home and stay there. This is not your world."

She turned away from Esther, toward a different path, and Esther, frustrated, threw a new ball after her.

"Are *you* looking forward to going home?"

Margaret paused, glanced back over her shoulder. "What?"

"To your husband."

"John..." Not the Earl of Hawton then. John Fortune was the husband she acknowledged.

"I'm sure he'll be glad you remember his name."

Something flashed in the other woman's eyes. "My husband is not the sort of man you ever forget anything about."

ω

The library was an interesting discovery. Nothing like the one she presumed she still slept in at the Hays' house, this was a tall, vaulted room containing far fewer books. However those there were looked bigger, and examination revealed them to be a mixture of manuscripts—many beautifully illuminated by hand—and printed books, all elegantly bound in leather or vellum.

They were on an amazing range of subjects: philosophy, mathematics, religious treatises, history, travel, astronomy, alchemy... Mostly they were in Latin, but some were Greek or Arabic, a few in what looked like English.

Taking a few to the polished table, she then wandered over to a chest at the back of the room. It opened easily enough. Inside, she found some sheets of paper and vellum, a couple of objects that looked like old fashioned school slates. Drago's name was carved at the top of one, Cosimo's on the other.

Thoughtfully, Esther put them back and picked up some of the loose, roughly cut sheets of paper. These she took to the table and sat to look at them. School work. Sums, hand-writing exercises, sentences that looked like grammar exercises, essays in Latin and in English. At the top of each was either Drago's or Cosimo's name.

Curiously, she compared the writing. Drago's was a bit of an untidy scrawl, as the comments in another hand—John Fortune's?—pointed out in the margin, but one made with sure, bold strokes. Cosimo's was elegant, perfectly formed if maybe over-decorative. Interestingly, more of his answers were marked as wrong. Nearly all of Drago's were correct.

"And what can you learn from these fascinating documents?"

She jumped visibly as his voice spoke at her shoulder. Everything inside her leapt too, sent her heart galloping loudly.

She said, "That you were a swot," and was grateful that her voice barely shook at all. She could feel his fingertips almost touching her nape, his warm breath on her hair.

He said, "I'm not sure what that is, but it sounds derogatory."

"It was meant to," she retorted, calmed by the humour in his voice. Curiously, she cast a glance over her shoulder, then wished she hadn't, for he was close, far too close as he leaned over her. Licking her suddenly dry lips, she said, "Tell me, what language is this written in?"

He reached around her, smoothing the paper she'd been examining. His arm brushed hers, rested warmly against it. He was wearing only the shirt he'd fought in, still streaked with blood and sweat. She could smell him, earth and spice and something unique forever associated in her mind with sex.

"Italian, of course. Are you mocking my handwriting?"

"No. It's just that...to me it's English."

"You've grown used to Italian by being here."

"I don't speak Italian. I only know three words."

"You're speaking it now."

She sighed. "I had a feeling you were going to say that."

"So how do you explain it?"

He sprawled across the table, so that he could see her face. There was a scratch along his jaw, surrounded by dried blood. It looked as if it grew out of his beard.

"Because Margaret's book is in English," she said slowly. "Everyone's *reported* to speak in Italian, but what's written is

English."

"This book that I'm meant to inhabit?"

"Yes." Without permission, a smile flickered across her lips. "But that's not right either, is it?"

"Naturally I believe it isn't."

It was difficult to concentrate when he was so close, his eyes steadily on hers. Making a manful effort, she frowned. "You and Cosimo were educated together. By John Fortune. You said...he taught you both...sorcery?"

"Among other things."

"Then Cosimo has similar powers to you?"

"No. He had no gift."

"But you did?"

He shrugged. "Enough to impress Fortune for a while."

"Just for a while?" It had been eating away at her—what exactly he could do with magic...

"After that I impressed him too much. He became afraid of me."

It wasn't a boast, a simple statement of fact. "Of a child?" she asked with deliberate scepticism. For some reason, she wanted to rile him, get beneath his skin.

"Of a child who grew too powerful to control. So while he still could, he worked on Cosimo."

A glimmer of understanding began to dawn. "You blame Fortune for your father's—choice of heir?"

"No, I blame my father for that." Abruptly, he swung himself off the table and onto the bench beside her. His warm thigh touched hers, burning her. It was a deliberate distraction, drawing her—or himself—away from things he didn't want to talk about or think about.

But Esther couldn't let it go there. Refusing to move to avoid his seductive touch, she said softly, "That's when I first saw you, isn't it? When your father passed you over for Cosimo."

"My father had passed me over for years. Another slight made no difference. When you appeared, I was devastated because one of the maids refused to sleep with me."

"Liar."

His lips curved into a smile, lazily reflected in his eyes. "You, on the other hand, had no difficulty at all with the sleeping."

"Ah." Esther flushed, and he moved his thigh against hers, causing the warm blood to flow even faster in her veins. Her brief domination was over.

"I'm not a vain man," Drago observed. "But even I am not used to women falling asleep on me just as I'm about to rock their world."

Laughter caught at her throat, half-embarrassed, half-hysterical. "As I recall, it was already rocked."

He waved one hand dismissively. "That was nothing. A taster. I had many, much more serious plans for you... I would have filled you with so much pleasure you wouldn't have been able to think or speak, only scream."

"I don't scream," she said shakily. His thigh pressed harder against hers. It was getting difficult to breathe evenly.

"You'd scream," he said positively, laying one warm, long hand thoughtfully on her upper thigh. "Don't you wish you'd tried harder to stay awake?"

"I—couldn't," she got out. "I wasn't really asleep. I just went back. I was *taken* back."

His hand, beginning to explore inward, paused. "Back?"

"To my own world. I don't choose it. When I come here, I appear to be asleep there. When I drop the book, or someone takes it from me, I wake up back there."

"And sleep here..."

"But even that doesn't follow. Because the first time, I vanished from your world completely. And when I came back here I was wearing my own clothes. I always go back in my own clothes. But now when I come here, my clothes are of this world. Or nonexistent. How is that?"

"I don't know." He stirred, idly caressing her thigh as he thought. "Do you think Fortune brought you here?"

"No...but I think he has something to do with this whole thing... Drago, what year is this?"

"The year of Our Lord fourteen hundred and ninety. What year is it to you?"

"Two thousand and seven," she said ruefully, but he didn't even blink. "But the point is, John Fortune doesn't actually live for another century from now. *Your* now. Or does he?"

She frowned with the effort of concentration, which was very difficult when Drago's hand softly kneaded her thigh, creeping inward and upward.

She swallowed. "In another hundred years, he'll write a book on necromancy. And mention something about a gateway to captured souls. Did he ever teach you about stuff like that? Do you know what he meant?"

"Souls...essence," he murmured, leaning into her. His breath kissed her face, his lips touched the corner of her mouth, causing her lips to part involuntarily, and withdrew. "He thought about that a lot, believed you didn't need to die and go to hell, that you could avoid the flames by taking your soul, your essence to another world. I didn't pay much attention to those bits. I was thirteen years old and I was going to live forever."

His hand turned, slid between her legs touching the throbbing, hot tenderness through the fabric of her gown, making her gasp. He seized the opportunity of her parted lips to cover them with his.

Against them, she whispered shakily, "I think that's what he's doing. Living forever, in your world. I think she is, too."

"Who?" he murmured, running his tongue along the length of her lips before slipping it between and sinking his mouth into hers. She clutched him, catching his hair in her fingers, surrendering to the kiss, returning it with passion because she could do nothing else.

"Who?" he repeated, when he came up for breath.

"Who what?"

"Who is also living forever in my world."

"Margaret. Matilda. Her name is really Margaret Marsden. I told you. She wrote a book in 1817 called *The Prince of Costanzo*, and I think it's the gateway to the souls somehow captured here. She disappeared from her own world, and I think she's been here ever since."

He drew back a little, looking at her. The flaring golden flames in his eyes began to die back, as if by an effort of will. Desperate to see them again, she wound her arms closer around his neck, slid her mouth down the line of his jaw to the corner of his mouth. He shivered, making her smile.

His hand caught the back of her head, his fingers tangling in her hair, holding her back when she would have kissed him.

"And you?"

"Me?"

"Why are you here?"

"By accident. I'm researching Margaret so that I can write a novel based on her life. I keep trying to read *The Prince of Costanzo* and ending up here." Abruptly, she remembered, and her hands fisted in his hair. "That's another thing! I think she took my ring."

"What ring?"

"The ring I was wearing when I came. I have to be wearing it or the book thing doesn't work. But when I woke up here this morning it was gone. Without it, I won't be able to come back."

Intense emotion flashed through his eyes as they searched hers. Before she could even begin to decipher it, he said, "Then you'd better make the most of the time you've got."

Chapter Ten

He leapt to his feet, his arms around her to drag her with him, crushing the length of her body into his. She gasped aloud at the warm, hard feel of him, the steel-like column of his cock pressing into her, and the realization that he was already so aroused sent a flood of new moisture cascading from her pussy. His mouth seized hers, ravaging, an implacable, irresistible force.

Not that she wanted to resist. Her mind may have objected to being seduced for whatever information he thought he was getting from her, but her body was more than willing and more than capable of overcoming her doubts. She opened her mouth to let him in, caressed his tongue wildly as it twisted around hers, fought back for domination of the kiss until he groaned deep in his throat and bent her backward across the table.

Coming up for air, he tugged once at the bodice of her gown and her breasts sprang free. Muttering something unintelligible, he fell on them like a starving man, his hand ravishing one while his mouth kissed and caressed the other, sucking, flicking her hard nipple with his tongue, rolling it in his mouth as his fingers squeezed the other.

Esther gave herself up to the tidal wave of sensation. Her hands moved of their own volition up and down his sweat-dampened back, burrowing underneath his shirt in search of bare skin, reaching down over his hard hips and muscular thighs as he ground his erection between her parted legs. Even with the annoyance of clothing between them, the movement of his hard cock against her desperate pussy was pushing her inexorably toward orgasm.

Remembering the last she had known with him, she moaned aloud with need, but she wanted him inside her this time. She wanted to bring him the same pleasure. "Now, please, now," she whispered, and he left off kissing her breasts to give a strange, breathless laugh as he captured her mouth instead.

Impatiently, he tugged up her skirts, bundling them carelessly around her waist. He thrust his hand between her thighs, giving a low groan as he found the pulsing heat of her pussy.

"Christ, you're this wet for me!" he muttered into her mouth. "I want to bathe in you... Tell me how much you want me."

"You already know."

"Tell me," he said fiercely.

"Lots," she babbled. "Lots and lots. Please, Drago..."

His fingers traced a teasing pattern around her petals, spreading her moisture around her central bud and the entrance to her body, without touching either.

"More than anyone else?"

"Christ, yes," she gasped, almost sobbing between laughter and tears of frustration. One sensitive finger glided across her clitoris and she cried out with the intensity of the pleasure, and then moaned as he slid it inside her. Her muscles clamped around it involuntarily. Then, deliberately, she squeezed tighter.

"I want you to remember me forever. Remember this."

Abruptly, his hand left her and she cried out at the loss.

But almost immediately, she felt it fumbling with his hose. She felt the blunt head of his cock sliding through her folds, burning, nudging at her entrance. She had seen it before. It was huge, far bigger than Kevin's, and it frightened her. Yet she had never wanted anything so much in her life as to feel it inside her.

"Will you?" he whispered against her lips.

"Oh God yes. Everything."

His eyes blazed into hers with fierce lust and triumph, but he didn't smile as he pushed inside her. She gasped as his cock stretched her, filling her with heat and a thousand sparks of intense pleasure. He pulled back, making her moan with the sensations scattering wildly through her whole body, then pushed back in further, surely the whole way. She felt as if he was in her womb. She arched up to meet him, to draw him even farther in and discovered she could. Moaning, she writhed under him, squeezed him, silently pleading with him to move, to fuck her.

He straightened slowly, so that he stood between her legs. Only then did he take his gaze away from her eyes, to look instead at where he entered her body. Esther looked, too, and nearly came at once. It was indescribably sexy to see the thick root of his cock impaling her, surrounded by his thatch of jet black hair and her lighter curls.

He pulled back slowly, revealing almost the full length of his big, veined shaft, only its head still hidden inside her. She moaned aloud. For a long moment, he held the position, breathing raggedly, watching her convulse around him. Then, deliberately, he thrust inside her and at her inarticulate sounds of pleasure, he smiled, wolfish, triumphant. He lifted her legs around his waist, and she cooperated with enthusiasm, locking her ankles together, drawing him deeper inside her, arching upwards, wriggling.

"You like that?" he panted.

"Christ yes, you know I do! Please, Drago..."

He slammed into her and she cried out with the ferocity of the pleasure.

"So you do," he observed, and did it again, thrusting inside her hard and fast and furious. The pleasure roared through her body, promising more joy than she could handle and yet she reached for it, strained for it.

Over the sounds of their panting breath, the moans and gasps and cries of delight, she became vaguely aware of footsteps.

"Someone's coming," she gasped, and almost laughed at her own joke, except the approaching orgasm was far too distracting.

"Who cares?" said Drago, and Esther jumped as something—someone—thudded into the library door.

A voice said, "It's locked." Arturo.

"Is it?" Esther whispered. Drago's eyes gleamed wickedly through the lust. He shook his head and drove into her again, faster than ever. Her fingers scrabbled at the table, seeking something to hold onto.

Another, older voice said impatiently, "I know he's in there."

Esther gave up. Orgasm crashed over her, convulsing her body, wracking it with helpless joy. It was wild, devastating and she couldn't have held it back for the world. And still he hammered her, thrusting in and out of her to extend the joy long beyond anything she had previously imagined before he finally released himself with a massive shout. Trembling, he collapsed on her, seizing her mouth, groaning into it as the orgasm tore through him. Hot jets of seed shot up inside her, setting off new pleasures, filling her with a satisfaction she had never known before.

Almost weeping under the onslaught of sensation and emotion, she didn't care that the people outside could hear him; she didn't even care if they came in. Nothing mattered beside this astounding, unstoppable pleasure, the amazing man who gave it to her, and took it.

Gradually, the wildness of his kiss changed, became more controlled in its sensual onslaught until he smiled against her lips.

"Well. It seems you're beautiful on the inside, too."

"Trust me, so are you," she said breathlessly, fervently, squeezing his cock which still felt more than beautiful inside her.

He gasped, gave another lazy thrust, just to show her who was boss, and she purred. More surreptitiously, she wiped the wetness of her face on to his shoulder.

"Tonight, after dinner, we'll do more of that," he promised. "Much more."

"After dinner?" Who needed dinner? Despite the massive orgasm, she was more than ready to go again. She wanted his body naked against her, entwined with her between the sheets for hours. Exciting as it was to be fucked on a table with her clothes on, she wanted to know more, so much more of him...

"With my new friend Alessandro de Verini among others. I'd like your help there. Shall I let them in?"

As he spoke he straightened, slowly withdrawing his cock from her body. Semen trickled down her thighs, which splayed helplessly on either side of him. He smiled at the sight of her, and suddenly the meaning of his words penetrated.

Leaping up, she squealed, "Not yet!"

Refastening his own clothes, he winked as she dragged her gown back over her breasts and shook it around her legs.

Arturo and an older man almost fell through the door, like bullets released from a gun.

Esther felt her jaw drop. Closing her mouth with an effort, she swallowed.

"How the hell did you do that?" she demanded.

Drago smiled beatifically. "Magic."

ω

Reaction had set in by the time she found the sanctuary of Drago's bedroom. Her legs trembled. Hell, everything trembled. She was so dizzy she felt sick, and the delicious ache between her legs had become more pain than pleasure. She didn't even know what had brought her here, except that it was the most familiar place she had in this world. And it was blessedly empty.

With relief she sank onto his luxurious bed. Part of her still felt exhilarated by the wild pleasure he'd given her, by the knowledge that she'd given him back something almost as good. But without his overwhelming presence, without the tender touch of his hands and the persuasion of his mouth, doubts and anxieties swamped her.

She didn't like being so helpless in the face of his physical attraction that she turned from a thinking, intelligent woman with considerable willpower into a gibbering heap of lustful jelly, uncaring even that he was using her much as she suspected he used Matilda—to gain information that might be useful to him.

Instead of remembering his kiss, the incredible force of the sexual pleasure he'd induced, she dwelled on her own weakness, on his careless neglect from the moment Arturo and his friend entered the library. In the face of their knowing smirks, he'd dismissed her like a whore who'd just completed her job to his satisfaction.

"Dinner will be in my private chamber," he'd said tersely, nodding significantly at the door. And she'd had no option but to leave like a dismissed servant. His semen trickled down her trembling legs as she walked, but she'd forced herself to hold her head high, to ignore the speculative gaze of the other men. But she couldn't block out their words as the door closed behind her.

The older man had said, "Why do you have to fuck your women in here? Can't you transact such business in bed like a Christian?"

"He likes being discovered *in flagrante*," Arturo mocked.

Esther fled, her whole body burning in shame. Not so much because of being discovered, but because of the fact that she was clearly not the only woman Drago had been discovered with. Other woman had inspired him with lust at least as urgent. And somehow their exciting encounter, the most amazing, beautiful thing that had ever happened to her, was reduced to one sordid, opportunistic screw among many.

Esther rolled over, burying her hot face in the pillow, fighting back the tears. She really wasn't much of a judge in matters of love: from the inertia of her relationship with Kevin to this insanity with a stranger she couldn't even begin to understand. But God help her, she wanted to.

The pillow smelled of him. Esther inhaled it like a drug, rubbed her cheek against the place his head had lain, and slowly sat up.

Invading someone's privacy by opening cupboards and

raking through drawers was anathema to her, but there was nothing to prevent her wandering around his room, looking. Actually *seeing* for the first time.

This, she realized, was his inner sanctum, which very few were privileged to enter. Only his most trusted servants came here, Lucrezia and Danilo. And her. He'd brought her here to interrogate her about her supposed magic, also intensely private to him...

Restlessly, she moved around the room, examining with new curiosity the scenes on the tapestries he'd chosen to decorate his bed chamber. One, stretched above his bed in surprisingly vivid reds and greens, was reminiscent of the famous Lady and the Unicorn, only here the shimmering magical creature was a white dragon, flames bursting from its open mouth, and it was flanked by a man as well as a woman. The man caressed the dragon with one hand; the other held a book with an astrological symbol. The woman, kneeling before the dragon, held a Bible.

Drago meant dragon. A magical man inspired—or hemmed in?—by knowledge and religion...

Esther wasn't sure what *her* fifteenth century Church would have made of this marriage of church, science and magic... Come to that, she wasn't sure what would be made of it here.

On the opposite wall was a battle scene, intricate and detailed, but only when she went up close to it did she realize that the sword of the central soldier seemed to shine, like the dragon. A magical sword? A sword of truth?

The final one was a hunting scene, another familiar tapestry subject, only this one was full of hunted animals. The hunters seemed almost incidental. Here at last, she found a unicorn, pitifully wounded. And again a white dragon, breathing fire from the air as a hail of arrows fell around it

Esther moved around the room, absorbing with her receptive new eyes every clue she could find. She picked up a beautiful miniature carving of a horse, running her fingers across its rippling muscles, the curve of its back. Laying it down, she moved to another of a naked woman. It, too, was perfectly formed, its luscious curves carved with appreciation and delight, its curiously expressive face gentle. Drago's perfect woman? Tender and sexy?

Another woman caught her eye. A small painted portrait in a carved gold frame, about four inches high. It stood on the table beside his bed, along with a leather-bound book in Latin that she couldn't read, though, oddly, the portrait's face was turned outward, away from the bed.

Picking it up, Esther saw that the woman was beautiful. Not luscious like the little statue, but fine featured, pale-skinned, her eyes large, beautiful and tragic. Her shoulders sloped elegantly into a gown of vivid red, only just modestly cut at the bosom.

Esther stared at the portrait. To all intents and purposes it was a bedside photograph. She had one of Kevin. Jealousy twisted through her, sharp as a knife. She had never seen the woman around the castle. Was she kept somewhere safer, less polluting, until she married him? Perhaps she was some foreign princess to whom he was betrothed...

The bedroom door opened with a click, and Esther spun 'round guiltily. Not Drago. Lucrezia. She didn't know whether she was more relieved or disappointed.

"There you are," Lucrezia said comfortably. "Let me help you prepare for the evening."

"Lucrezia, who is this?"

"Ah. That's the princess Beatrice." Lucrezia bustled over to gaze at the picture over Esther's arm. "Beautiful, isn't she?"

"Yes..." She licked her dry lips, said quickly, "Why does he keep this beside his bed?"

Lucrezia shrugged. "To remember her, I suppose. Though you'll have noticed he turned her face away from the bed."

"Why is that?" she asked, feeling the blush rise into her cheeks. "So she can't see what he gets up to in there?"

Lucrezia laughed comfortably. "I expect so. The idea of your mother watching your bedroom antics can't be a comfortable one."

"His *mother*?"

Startled, she looked again, could discern a certain resemblance in the shape of her face, her eyes.

Lucrezia laughed again. "Were you imagining it was his wife?" Amused, she took the portrait from Esther, laid it back where it had been, facing away from the bed.

"Well, his betrothed or someone," Esther said ruefully.

"He isn't," Lucrezia said, and when she blinked, explained, "He isn't betrothed yet. There are some long-running negotiations over a German princess, but they've been postponed, apparently, till after the trouble with Cosimo is sorted out. If you ask me, it was a relief to Drago."

It was quite a relief to Esther, too, for reasons she couldn't quite come to grips with. She sank back onto the bed.

Lucrezia said, "I'll tell him you were jealous, though—he'll like that."

"Don't!" Esther said, alarmed. "I'm not. I'm just curious." She frowned, flicking a quick glance at the other woman. "What do you mean, 'he'll like that'?"

Lucrezia gave a sly smile.

Esther said flatly, "He likes attention, doesn't he?"

151

"He'd certainly like yours."

Esther's gaze flew back to her without permission and for a moment, the two women stared at each other. Then Lucrezia moved and sat on the bed beside her.

"Have you not worked that much out? You sit here all churned up, worrying about other women—much as he does about you and other men. Do you not know that he has waited ten years for you?"

Her heart thudded, tried to climb out of her throat. "For *me*?" she whispered.

"He saw you, in his room upstairs, where Rudolfo had banished him when his mother died. Tore the castle apart looking for you, described every inch of you to me. Something about you got under his skin. He wouldn't accept that you were a dream, not even years later. He stopped talking about you, even to me, but I know he thought of you still. And then, when he finally found you... I haven't seen him so elated, so disturbed, so afraid of doing the wrong thing, not since he was a child. Not even then. *So you must not let him down!*"

Esther blinked, still trying to comprehend this. "Let him down?" she repeated stupidly.

"He wants to rely on you, and if you're not worthy..." For the first time since they'd met, there was a threat in Lucrezia's voice, quickly softened by a squeeze of the hand. "Lady, he's like my son and I love him more than life. Don't hurt him."

"Hurt him? I couldn't."

Lucrezia stared at her. "He's different, isn't he? A little strange, but still he fascinates you. Yet you're afraid of him. Just remember this—he's at least as afraid of you."

"But then I'm afraid of everyone," said Drago from the door, making both women jump up from the bed. He stood in the doorway, leaning one shoulder against the frame, still in his blood-stained shirt. "Especially her," he added, nodding at Lucrezia. "Go away, you old witch."

Lucrezia, apparently seeing no insult in this mode of address, merely smiled and walked past him out of the room. Drago straightened and closed the door behind her. Otherwise, neither he nor Esther moved, simply stared at each other over the floor space.

Esther said lightly, "Is she?"

"A witch? No. I'm the witch here, remember?"

"And usurper and tyrant, yadda-yadda-yadda."

He smiled faintly and began to walk toward her. He came to a halt, one foot on the step leading up to the bed, and looked into her face.

"What was that all about, anyway? Did I offend you by taking you on the library table?"

Esther flushed. In spite of herself, her loins began to tingle dangerously. "No. If I was offended, it was because I felt like a whore dismissed after servicing you."

"I was being chivalrous. I thought you wanted to escape."

"Oh I did! If only to avoid hearing myself discussed."

Still he came no closer, didn't touch her. "You won't be so discussed again. I made some mistakes, trying to make you think I didn't care. I never meant that to lead anyone to disrespect you. I often behave badly. But for what it's worth, I've never taken any other woman on the library table."

"Will you stop saying that?"

His lips quirked. "What? 'Taking you on the library table'? I like the way you blush when I say it."

"Yes, well don't lie about it," she blustered. "I heard quite enough to know I'm *not* the only one so honoured."

"There were a couple of incidents in corridors. And behind

153

a screen during a banquet. And I fell out of a tree once with the blacksmith's daughter. But I was much younger then. And you're the only one I—"

"—took on the library table. Okay, I get it." She sat on the bed with a bump.

He smiled, making the golden flames leap in his eyes, and came up the steps to sit beside her.

"I loved your face," he said conversationally. "When I first saw you. Strong, beautiful, humorous, insatiably curious, sensual...and while I couldn't bear it, I even loved your compassion. You were too vivid, too alive to have been a dream, even the dream of a deranged adolescent. It was your face that kept me sane through the difficulties of those years, gave me purpose, made me strong when I was tempted to weaken. I was sorry for frightening you, for you were my talisman, although as time passed, I never expected to see you again.

"When I finally found you, I knew the fantasy I'd made up wasn't real. The true woman was so much more... I needed to fascinate you, make you love me while avoiding the hurt of loving you. I was afraid I couldn't make you stay. And I can't, can I?"

Esther's heart beat loudly. Afraid to touch him, she said hoarsely, "No." His lips quirked upwards without humour. He looked away. More strongly, Esther said, "I need the ring to come back. I won't even get near the book again after today."

He looked upward, at the ceiling. "I don't know if that's true. *She* came back without the ring. Matilda. If she hadn't, you wouldn't have the ring, would you?"

"She said she'd become part of this world..."

"But you haven't."

Closing her eyes because it was the only way she dared, she slowly laid her cheek on his shoulder. "I don't know. When

I'm here, you are my world. When I'm there..." Tears pressed at her eyes, tugged at her throat. "...you are my world, too."

He was very still. Very silent.

A knock came at the door and still he didn't answer. Danilo called, "Sir, your guests are on their way."

"Thank you."

His hands lifted her head, his thumb brushed the wetness on her cheek. "There is a passage between our worlds," he whispered. "If we want it enough, we can use it."

She opened her eyes into his intense gaze. With something like wonder, she reached up and touched the hand on her cheek, pressed it to her skin.

He said, "In my heart, you have always been my wife."

Esther barely heard the door open, Lucrezia's bustling. "Enough now, sir, go and join your guests. Let me dress the lady to your credit and hers."

As if he hadn't heard either, Drago twisted his hand in her hold until their fingers were intertwined. His smile was soft, as if he wasn't even aware of it.

He said, "I think we understand each other a little better."

"Sir," Lucrezia warned

"All right, all right, I'm going. Don't bully *her* or I'll dismiss you."

Lucrezia snorted. Their hands separated reluctantly and Drago stood, tearing off his shirt as he went.

Dazed, warm with happiness that seemed to have sprung from nowhere, Esther watched the muscles ripple up his naked back as he bent to retrieve a fresh shirt from the chest. Her loins stirred lazily, reminding her of the hot, urgent joy of the library table. From another chest, he pulled out a dark blue silk tunic, apparently at random and cast a quick grin at her over his shoulder as he departed.

Chapter Eleven

Esther stared at herself in Drago's large, ornately framed mirror. Lucrezia had brushed her blonde hair until it shone with golden lights, then tied it into a clever chignon that somehow made her appear prettier, emphasizing the heart shape of her face and the delicacy of her features. Even her neck looked longer than usual and considerably more elegant, though that might have had something to do with the stunning necklace of milky white pearls that Lucrezia had just clasped around it. Somehow the jewellery transformed the low-cut red whore's dress into an elegant evening gown. She would still have to be careful about leaning forward in case her breasts tumbled out, but this time, somehow, she felt beautiful...

"In my heart, you have always been my wife."

In under a day, by her own reckoning, she had gone from breaking one engagement to...whatever this was. And the irony was, with Drago she didn't give a damn about marriage. The engagement to Kevin had been important to her because it was an acknowledgement that someone needed her, had committed to her. The wrong reason to marry anyone, of course, and she should never have done it, but Drago...Drago blew her away and she just wanted to be with him all the time under any and all circumstances.

Almost fearfully, she touched the cool, smooth pearls at her breast, caressing them.

"I can't wear these," she said with genuine regret. "They're not mine."

"They are his to give," Lucrezia said sternly. "They belonged to his mother."

Esther dropped her hand, staring at the other woman. Lucrezia's gaze softened again. "He wants you to have them, to wear them tonight. And it's not just one of his games—it is for you. A gift. Which also states his claim and lifts your status in the eyes of any who might have thought...otherwise, from his previous behaviour."

Lucrezia gave a rueful, slightly twisted smile. "His behaviour is often bad, but he is not a bad man. You understand the difference?"

Esther nodded. She couldn't speak for the lump in her throat and she didn't want the silly tears to come now and stain whatever Lucrezia had done with her face to make it look so smooth and radiant. Certainly, she hadn't used any cosmetics, merely hot and cold rose-scented water.

It was happiness, Esther thought with amazement as she walked toward the door. Because of Drago's words. New warmth and excitement filled her, flooded her and shone out of her eyes, her mouth, her very pores.

Now you're being fanciful, not to say ridiculous. Get a grip, woman, or you'll be no use at all to him in there.

Exactly what he expected of her, she wasn't sure, but he had requested her help in binding Alessandro to him more securely, and she was more than happy to help in that.

"Madonna," Lucrezia said as she reached for the handle. Esther glanced at her. She winked and grinned, startlingly like Drago. "You are beautiful."

Taking a deep breath, Esther sailed through the open door and into another unknown.

ω

Drago broke off in mid-sentence and stared at her. Elation coursed through him, because she wore the dress and the pearls and she was the most beautiful creature he had ever seen. He had been right to stop playing, to take off the mask and trust her. He had won more in that brief ten minutes of talk than in all their previous encounters put together.

Although the astounding sex in the library had probably softened her up.

It had the opposite effect on him. Surreptitiously, he adjusted his hose under the table to accommodate the wayward growth of his cock before rising from the table and going to meet her.

Everyone else in the room had fallen silent, too, staring at the girl. Some were caught by her beauty, he knew, others waited to take their lead from him. Although the pearls should have given them all the clue they needed. Before the end of the night, the fact that she had worn them would be all over the court, and round the rest of the country by tomorrow.

Which was just as well. He needed her position secure before he left in the morning. And tonight, while she slept, he would make doubly sure of her safety with protective spells. Although he didn't think Matilda presented much threat to her—his stepsister would assume she'd be out of the way forever the next time she faded to her own world. After all, Esther hadn't been here for long. Drago could only hope he had bound her enough...and take Matilda away with him in the morning. Threat or no threat, the woman was poison.

Well, it was time, long past time, to cut the poison out of his realm. For good, if he could. Once he had thought no other revenge would do. Exquisite revenge no longer seemed necessary. Straightforward brutality would do just as well.

It all seemed strangely trivial now, the desire for revenge which had once consumed him. And the reason for that stood right in front of him—his salvation, his future, and that of Costanzo.

As he took her hand, Esther gave him a quick, oddly shy smile that enchanted him. Her eyes were radiant and the astounding knowledge hit him like a blow. He had made someone happy.

He couldn't help it. He laughed. No doubt it would add to the legend of his insanity, but he didn't care, especially as the responsive twinkle lit Esther's eyes once more. He loved that about her. There didn't need to be a reason understandable to anyone else, but she shared every tiny shift in his moods.

He kissed her hand with civil respect. This time, the discreet flick of his tongue on her skin was for Esther's perception alone, and he had his reward in the quick catch of her breath.

Straightening immediately, he led her toward the table, which had been covered with heavily embroidered linen and laid with silver plate and gleaming, heavy cutlery and glass goblets. His male guests were already standing. Julia rose, too, giving the signal to the other women. Even Matilda, smiling without expression, got to her feet.

"I'm not sure if you know all of our guests," Drago said easily. "I have been remiss in formal presentations. Lady Esther, this is Father Luca, my friend and confessor."

Confessor was a formal title. Friend he was and for that

reason, Drago could hardly burden him with all his sins, especially those heresies the Church hated most. Luca bowed and let his severe face relax into a genuine smile that Esther returned.

"Count and Countess de Gallio." Mischievously, Drago watched her reaction, since the last time she had met the count had been in the library. Only by his own hasty spell had Drago prevented him witnessing the consummation of their passion.

"Madonna Julia di Ripoli, Arturo's sister, and my own sister Matilda you already know."

With natural grace, Esther accepted the introductions and exchanged greetings. Only as he was about to move on did a flash of reflected candlelight attract his attention to Matilda's hand. She wore a lapis lazuli ring. Drago didn't pay much attention to jewellery, but this ring he had seen before, and not just on Esther's finger.

Now what was his thrice-damned sister up to?

Esther's hand went rigid in his. Her gaze flicked up from Matilda's ring to her eyes, and held. Matilda smiled. Drago could have slapped her. He really didn't want this quarrel now. But Matilda seemed determined to provoke it. He couldn't quite work out why, unless to encourage Esther to make a fool of herself and lose credibility. But one thing he did know: whatever she wanted Esther to believe, she hadn't stolen Esther's ring from his bed chamber. She couldn't have. There was far too much magical protection surrounding it.

So this was Matilda's own ring, which had come with her from her first world. So where was Esther's? Did it remain in that world, refusing to be part of his? After all, there was only one object, existing in two worlds. It couldn't exist *twice* in one of them.

He tightened his grip on Esther's hand, warning.

But it seemed he underestimated his love. She simply nodded distantly at Matilda and turned to the man next to her.

Good girl! He let his thumb stroke the soft skin between her fingers, felt her instant shiver of response and grew uncomfortably harder. He just had to get through this evening, and then there was all night to make love to her, to know that delectably hot and passionate little body from lips to toes...

He had known all these years ago, even with his limited experience, that her outwardly gentle face promised spectacular sensuality, a passion only half-awakened, he guessed, before he'd begun to seduce her last night. Before, unable to wait, he'd taken her so fiercely in the library and known her equally urgent response. He could feel all over again, her hands and nails scrabbling frantically on his back, her writhing body pushing up into him, gathering him in...

Stop there, Drago, concentrate...!

"Messire Nicholas Console," he said blandly, "the renowned astronomer from Florence, who is kind enough to share his time and his knowledge with us this month. And of course, Count Alessandro de Verini."

You wouldn't have known Alessandro had been in prison, or that he'd been inches away from death by combat that morning. Dressed in largely borrowed finery, he looked every inch the courtier. Only in the very stillness of his body did he betray his discomfort, and in the slightly fixed nature of his smile could you see a hint of tension. Drago expected that. The man was surrounded by loyal Drago supporters who reviled him as a traitor. And across the table from him sat Matilda, Fortune's wife, who surely regarded him as a traitor now, for to all intents and purposes, Drago had won him back.

But Drago had no intention of letting them discuss war or rebellion. Not yet, anyway. As the food was served, he led the conversation on neutral things, kept it light and witty, occasionally learned, until Alessandro began to relax. Wine flowed, and conversation split. While Drago caught up with his old friend Countess de Gallio, he deliberately listened in to the conversation going on between Esther and Alessandro on his other side. She had a quiet yet exotic charm that he was sure Alessandro was not immune to. She also had an inner calmness, a stability that Drago lacked and that he knew Alessandro would notice. Esther was his other half, making him whole as a man and as a ruler, and he wanted Alessandro, the whole world, to see that. He wanted Esther to see it, too, for he was fairly sure it worked both ways, that he made her whole, too.

Fierce pride rose in him afresh. Intensely aware of her warmth beside him, not touching, he could smell the faint rose and vanilla scent of her skin. For a while, he tortured himself pleasurably with the knowledge that he could touch her when he wanted to, that she was his. And then, eventually, he gave in and reached for her beneath the tablecloth, resting his palm on her warm thigh.

Her leg jumped at his touch. There was a subtle change in her breathing, but she neither moved away nor broke off her conversation with Alessandro. Instead, she moved her leg subtly under his hand, caressing him back.

Drago was not and never would be a moderate man. He was used to extremes of emotion, was no stranger to consuming lust—although this desire for Esther was even more consuming than most. What truly scared him was the power of the warm feeling behind it, the need to protect and cherish, simply to *be* with.

Unable to resist, Drago slid his hand around her leg and upward. Her heat almost unmanned him. His cock was so hard it was painful, but he couldn't stop. Her body tensed, as if to resist the sensations he was deliberately inspiring, but still she didn't push him away. Using the side of his hand like a knife, he sliced slowly between her legs, stroking over and over. He felt the flood of new moisture burning his hand, heard her swallow audibly, give a tiny cough to cover up.

"Of course," he murmured to Countess de Gallio. He wondered if he could make Esther climax, just by stroking through the fabric of her gown in a room full of guests. Would she be able to hide it? Was it cruel to try? His finger probed more intimately, making her lick her lips. He heard the sound of her tongue quite clearly, and smiled. Countess de Gallio looked slightly surprised, but carried on talking. No wonder the count rarely went home.

But he wasn't thinking about the countess. He was thinking about Esther, her lips and tongue and what he would like them to do to his burning body right now. While he continued to stroke her, his wayward imagination moved on. He had just got to her lips wrapping round the head of his cock, when something firm took hold of it in reality.

Esther's hand, under the table like his, grasping his cock as if she knew exactly what she was doing, exactly what he wanted. Drago sighed in bliss.

"Exactly!" said Countess de Gallio, apparently pleased, and returned to her meal.

Drago picked up his glass and sipped the rich red wine while the amazing woman by his side stroked his cock under the table, making him forget everything and everyone else. There was only Esther's hand and Esther's womanhood pulsing under his touch and the wine burning down his throat to cool him...

He laid down his glass. Moderate drinking, to facilitate the immoderate loving of the night to come... Later.

Concentrate, Drago.

She turned to him, her eyes glowing, and as she parted her lips—to speak, to climax, he didn't know which. He just wanted to cover them with his and kiss her till she moaned. And then he wanted them wrapped around his surging cock, wondered if she would, if he would have to teach her. Judging by what she was doing now, he guessed not. She hadn't come to him a virgin. Although she hadn't said anything, he suspected that sexual mores were different in her world. He wondered if there was a man there he was sharing her with. Drago saw his knuckles whiten around the stem of his glass and deliberately relaxed.

His hand stilled between her thighs. So did hers on his cock. A taster of the night. It was so much better to wait, to anticipate.

Only slightly shakily, she said, "Count de Verini is offering to show me the Church of Santa Maria tomorrow."

Oh is he?

"The glass is very beautiful," he allowed, "and the statue of the Virgin exquisite. However, I think it will have to be another day."

"How so?" Alessandro asked, leaning forward to see past Esther to him. As if frightened he would be able to discern what was going on between them, she snatched her hand away from Drago's cock, and he could have yelled with vexation. But Alessandro wasn't being insolent, merely curious. And Drago, after all, had been waiting for the opportunity.

He was a ruling prince, not a carefree youth in the throes of his first sexual crush.

Pulling himself together he said casually, "I thought you might prefer to ride with me tomorrow. We go to return my sister to her husband."

A sudden silence swept the room, broken only by the faint tinkle of glass against plate as Matilda laid down her wine.

"Does my husband know?" she drawled, her voice, her expression, so carefully humorous that he knew he'd surprised her. As if she'd genuinely believed he was succumbing to her charms, when in reality he'd sooner embrace a snake.

"Fortune? I'm sure he will before the night is done."

"You have sent a messenger?"

Drago smiled at her. "Why should I risk another man? You tell him."

Matilda cast a quick glance she could not prevent at Luca the priest. "Tell him what? I have no details and no time to reach him by messenger."

"The village of Monteverini at midday. He'll be there."

Esther was staring at him.

So was Alessandro. "*My* village?"

"You want it back, don't you?" He didn't look at Alessandro, but at Matilda. He was amused that she seemed to be struggling to absorb the fact that he knew she could communicate with Fortune without messenger or paper. Not complicated ideas, perhaps, but straightforward concepts like times and places and who would be there. When Fortune had taught him, Drago had never told his teacher that it was something he could already do. With certain people.

De Gallio said uneasily, "This isn't wise, sir. If he knows you will be there, Cosimo will lay a trap for us."

"What, when my sister is with us? She is our shield."

"With respect, sir, they know you will protect her," Alessandro protested. "She has been here with you unharmed for a month. I'm afraid they will take the chance and attack!"

Drago shrugged. "There will be enough men to watch our

backs," he said carelessly.

"Make him come *here* for the Lady Matilda," the Count de Gallio urged. "At least then it is on our terms!"

"But we wouldn't get Monteverini back for Alessandro, would we?"

"But do we know *Alessandro* will keep Monteverini for you?"

"Oh I think so," said Drago easily. He was aware of Alessandro's flush of shame and anger. "He was lied to by people he trusted. Now he has seen the truth for himself and can make his own judgment."

"In a day?" asked Julia scathingly.

"Well, I think it has been rather longer than a day. I will vouch for Alessandro's loyalty. Not least because if it turns out I am wrong, I will kill him." Drago smiled serenely over their heads to the window. "It is a beautiful, clear night," he observed into the sudden silence. "Messire Colone, is there something interesting in the sky to show us? I've set up the glass you brought..."

Colone was more than willing to expound his pet subject, and as Drago and he went over to the window to look at the stars, the others took the opportunity to move into huddles, whispering, no doubt, about tomorrow. Drago didn't trouble to listen in. Right now he was more interested in what Colone was saying. Only Esther distracted him, standing behind him while he looked through Colone's glass. Though she gazed at the sky, he was aware of her willing him to look at her, to speak to her. Her body still shrieked with the sexual tension he had induced—so did his—but beneath it was a deeper concern.

And so, quicker than he would normally have done so, he graciously gave up his place to Alessandro and stepped back close to Esther.

"Is this safe, what you are doing?" she demanded anxiously.

"Oh yes."

To his surprise, she gave a half-laugh. "Why do I believe everything you tell me? When do we leave?"

He interlaced his fingers with hers. "I leave at dawn. You—don't."

Her fingers convulsed around his, though her gaze didn't leave the sky. "Let me come, Drago. I don't know how long I've got."

"I can't risk you. Fortune wants you. He thinks I'm bringing you with Matilda—that's why I know he'll come. But you must stay here, protected."

"And when you come back, I'll be gone."

Her grief tore into him, bringing with it a stabbing pain in his stomach. Ignoring it, he said firmly, "No. I won't believe that."

"And if it's true? Can't we spend every possible moment together before I'm taken back?"

He returned the pressure of her fingers. "Only every *possible* moment. We have tonight."

Her breath caught at that, as he knew it would, but his triumph was dampened by her sorrow which amounted to desperation. It made his head ache.

"Esther, I will find..."

Abruptly, she tugged her hand free and walked away.

Drago was not used to such treatment. He thought he should probably be angry. Instead, he found pride warring with laughter. After ten years longing for the strange lady of his "dream", the reality was so different, so much better than anything his imagination had conjured...

And yet he didn't like her being upset. It upset him. That, too, was a novelty. As the Count de Gallio came up to him and he spoke his low-voiced reassurance, his request to care for Esther in his absence, he saw her go directly up to Matilda.

Vaguely alarmed, he invoked his gift, so that while he spoke to the count, his hearing expanded until unbearable noise filled his ears, his entire head, temporarily blotting out the count's anxiety. Quickly, he filtered out the background until he could hear Esther speaking abruptly to Matilda.

"Please give me my ring back," she demanded, and unexpected warmth flooded Drago. She wasn't angry with him, just determined to get back to him. It felt like a gift. Somewhere in this life or a previous one, he must have done something right...

Matilda smiled. "*My* ring," she said gently. "As you may have noticed, I'm not dead, so it is still mine."

"You don't *need* it!"

"But you do." Matilda's smile broadened, like a weasel's, and for the first time alarm bells began to ring in Drago's head. He had seen that look before. She wasn't ready to go back to Fortune, and Drago had taken it out of her hands. She didn't like that. It made her dangerous...

She drawled, "My dear, you're becoming a bore and I want you gone. I don't need a dynasty of little Dragos complicating my plans. And frankly, I don't need my husband distracted by his fascination with whatever you can tell him about your world."

"Then you won't give me it? I could take it."

Matilda's smile faded to curiosity. Drago shared it, for there was steel in Esther's quiet voice. But he was becoming distracted. Filtering was difficult, concentrating on the Count de Gallio almost impossible, for his aching head had begun to spin. A sick feeling began to gnaw at his gut.

He had never associated physical violence with Esther before, but suddenly he realized he had no real idea exactly what she was capable of. Perhaps Matilda had the same thoughts, for she laughed, idly rubbing her fingers together. If Drago hadn't been watching intently he would have missed it. The ring came off her finger, was speedily passed into Esther's hands.

Drago frowned. She shouldn't have done that. The ring was Matilda's, not Esther's, so why give it to her?

"Perhaps," Matilda allowed. "But as you see, there's no need. I don't want it any more. I'll even drink with you. To family."

As she spoke, she reached across the table to pick up her own and Esther's glasses, pressed one into Esther's slightly stunned hand. She clearly hadn't expected so easy a victory. Neither had Drago, and it bothered him, only his head seemed suddenly too sluggish to think. He shook it.

Matilda lifted the glass to her lips. The ring on Esther's finger glinted in the candle-light as she raised her glass.

Noise exploded in Drago's head. *"I don't want it anymore."*

He tried to speak, to run across the room to dash the glass from Esther's hand, but he couldn't move. As the glass touched her lips, Matilda looked straight into his eyes and smiled.

With a roar of effort, Drago launched himself across the room. But the wine was in Esther's mouth. She swallowed it in a gulp that made her choke as she watched him in amazement.

Drago smacked the glass from Esther's hand, heard the tinkle of a thousand shards on the floor as if it was an exploding gun, and then, unable to prevent it any longer, he sank to his knees.

"Drago! Drago!" Desperate fear in her beautiful voice, Esther fell with him, her arms around him. "What is it, what's happened?"

"As if you don't know," Matilda cried shrilly. "You've poisoned him! Just because he would not marry you! Get away from my brother!"

And Matilda was there at his other ear, whispering. "I've got you both, one way or another. You lose, Drago."

Drago, willing strength back into his pain-wracked body, stared into Esther's eyes. "Be sick. Make yourself sick. Purge." He had no idea if he said the words aloud, or if she could pick up the speech of his mind.

"Count de Gallio, take her ring," Matilda commanded. "It has a secret compartment. My God, she's poisoned my brother with whatever is in there! To think that a kinswoman of mine...! He may have been a usurper, poor misguided boy, but he did not deserve *this*!"

"No," Esther cried out in furious panic. "No, no, no, no...!"

The poison had got to her. Her fingers dug into his shoulders with the pain of it. *Oh Jesus, Mary and Joseph I cannot lose her now...*

And the agony of that was so great, beyond anything he felt in his gut or his head, that he roared out with her, a long, mindless cry of grief.

Chapter Twelve

Still struggling, Esther cried out in rage as the Hays' library swung into focus. The book lay on the desk in front of her, her naked hand lying palm down on one of the pages.

She registered the absence of the ring an instant before she realized she was not alone. Beside her stood Kevin and his friend Steve, and facing them, holding Esther's ring in nerveless fingers, Lady Hay. All three of them were staring at her, open-mouthed.

"Good grief, Esther, that must have been some dream," Kevin remarked. There was a sneer behind the amusement in his voice, but she had no time to think about that.

Pleading, she stretched out her hand to Lady Hay. "Give me it quickly! I have to get back, he's dying!"

"Esther, snap out of it," Kevin commanded. "You were dreaming."

Esther jumped to her feet, snatching for the ring. Alarmed, Lady Hay stepped back out of her reach, and Esther had a sudden glimpse of how she must appear: wild, demented, tears of fury and grief pouring down her cheeks.

Esther let her arm fall back to her side. "Please," she whispered. "Give me the ring, let me go back."

Lady Hay's frown changed from anxiety to puzzlement.

"Back where?"

"What's going on?"

All heads whipped around to face the door, where Sir Ian stood, gazing without cordiality at his wife.

Lady Hay was not quite pleased, not quite comfortable. "Nothing, dear. Merely, Kevin and Esther have sold me the ring..."

"*Sold?*" Esther stared at Kevin. "It's not yours to sell."

"We decided last night, remember?" Kevin wouldn't look at her. He was smiling from Lady Hay to her husband. "When we're married, we'll share everything."

"But we're not getting married, Kevin. *That's* what we decided last night."

"A lover's tiff," Kevin said smoothly. "I talked to Steve about it and I realized you didn't mean it, so I came back. This is the perfect way for us to start afresh—*without* your hang-ups about the past, and *with* a nice nest egg in the bank."

"Nicely thought out, Kevin." Esther's voice was small and hard, thick with sarcasm. And yet not quite steady. "There's just one problem—the ring is mine. And I'm not selling."

"My dear, you've already sold," said Lady Hay. "Your fiancé has my cheque, I have your ring and your receipt."

"But I haven't agreed to this. He *can't* sell what isn't his. I want my ring back now. Kevin, give her back the cheque."

"You're in no state to discuss this now, Esther. Let's just go." Kevin took her arm purposefully, but she shook him off.

"I'm not going anywhere without my ring."

"Esther..."

"I'm serious. Lady Hay?"

Lady Hay's glance flickered from her to her husband. Then

she shook her head. "He has my cheque. I keep the ring."

"Then you're stealing from me, and he's stealing from you." Furiously, Esther delved inside her bag for her phone. Why couldn't they see there was no *time* for this? "The police can sort it out."

"Come now, there's no need for that." Sir Ian took command, walking into the room at last. "Let's talk about it. Kevin, show Esther the cheque."

With something akin to pride, Kevin waved the piece of paper in her face. Esther pushed it aside. She didn't even look at it.

"There's no crime," Sir Ian said, sounding careless, even faintly amused. His wife looked relieved. "Merely a transaction from which you are now trying to withdraw."

Of course, now Hay had the set, book and ring. He could investigate at his leisure. She didn't have that leisure; neither did Drago.

"I can't withdraw from something I had no part in," Esther snapped.

"Lawyers won't see it that way," Hay said mildly.

Esther stared at him. "*You*'re threatening *me* with lawyers?"

"Not threatening. I'm just reminding you that my lawyers are better than yours."

He spoke with humour, deliberately reminiscent of a boastful little boy. No one laughed. Again, Kevin took her elbow, but this time when she tried to shake him off, he held firm, and on her other side, Steve materialized, grasping her arm in a grip that deliberately hurt.

"Let's go," he said in her ear. "Don't you *dare* make a fool of him again."

"I don't care about him," Esther said wildly. There was only

Drago, dying in that other world, alone without her, perhaps believing *she* was dead. "Sir Ian, please. We can talk about ownership later, please just let me have the book and the ring for the afternoon—please!"

They'd started to drag her off, despite her desperate struggles. She got in a couple of good kicks on their shins that made them wince in harmony.

"You were asleep," Lady Hay said coldly. "I'd say your research was over."

"I'm afraid I have to agree," Sir Ian said blandly. "Goodbye, Esther, it's been a pleasure having you here."

There was nothing she could do. Digging her heels literally into the carpet, struggling wildly in the grip of the two men could not halt her inexorable progress toward the door for long.

"Drago," she whispered, straining to gaze over her shoulder at the open book on the table. Fresh tears coursed down her cheeks. "Drago..."

The hazy print on the pages fuzzed further under her stricken gaze. It seemed to funnel upwards, making her blink, forming into a...

Her heart leapt into her throat. Lady Hay cried, "Jesus Christ! Ian! *Ian!*"

"What the...?" Hay stared, mouth open. Kevin and Steve, distracted at last from their single-minded mission to get her out of the house, turned and gawped.

The funnel formed into a whirlwind, spinning itself into the unmistakable formation of a man. A man in leggings and a dark blue silk tunic, a sword and dagger dangling from the ornate belt at his hip. He moved smoothly out of the book, already reaching out for Esther.

His hands were warm and solid on her face, his mouth

already covering hers before he was even fully formed. Like magic, the restricting grip on her arms fell away and she could hold him, revel in him.

"You're alive, you're alive! Are you alive there, too?" she breathed incoherently into his mouth. "I thought you were dying. She poisoned your wine, from my ring..."

"Yes, she did. But for obvious reasons I have deliberately built up a tolerance to most poisons. It's quite hard to kill me that way. And she didn't poison you. She only pretended, to spite me. She wanted me to die believing she'd killed you, too. In either world. And if you'd remained in my world, you would have been blamed for poisoning me. Or so she thought. That's why she gave you the ring."

"Cow," Esther said, but quite without rancour, almost blissfully. The only important thing in either world was that he lived...

Eyes tightly closed, she pressed her cheek to his, loved the warm roughness of his skin, his beard.

From a long way off, she heard Steve's voice.

"Who the *fuck* is this?" Fear as well as astonishment was making him bluster. God knew how it would affect Kevin.

Drago stilled for an instant, as if returning to his surroundings, remembering the position he'd found her in. He lifted his head, dropped his right arm while his left slid quickly to her waist, drawing her to his side farthest from the others.

"I am Drago, Prince of Costanzo," he said mildly. "Who the—er—fuck—are you?"

"Bradshaw, Steve Bradshaw. Kevin's mate." His hand waved toward Kevin with an odd mixture of triumph and aggression.

Drago merely blinked. "His *mate*?"

"Friend," Esther translated quickly.

"And I'm *her* fiancé," Kevin added aggressively. "So take your hands off her."

Once this uncharacteristic possessiveness might have impressed her. Now she found herself thinking dispassionately that both he and Steve appeared to be blocking the fact that Drago, resplendent in Renaissance costume, had just walked out of a book on Sir Ian Hay's table. But it was a very fleeting thought because Drago's fingers at her waist tightened convulsively at Kevin's words, and then fell away leaving her cold.

"You are betrothed?" he said without expression.

"Not anymore," Esther said quickly. "I broke it off last night."

"We've already said that was a tiff," Kevin interrupted with a hint of desperation. "Esther, get over here, we're leaving."

"Goodbye," said Esther frostily. "Leave Lady Hay's cheque on your way out."

Kevin made a sudden lunge for her. After all, he couldn't risk Lady Hay returning the ring and stopping the cheque. But before Esther could as much as back away, there was a screech of steel, a flash of motion and Drago held his sword point to Kevin's throat.

Kevin, poorly balanced and terrified to move, looked wildly into Drago's suddenly ferocious eyes.

"I'll kill you if you touch her." Amazingly, there was a wealth of pain behind Drago's threat. Her relationship with Kevin truly hurt him.

Esther said softly, "I chose you, Drago." And for the first time she considered the possibility that this might be almost as astounding as Drago choosing her.

"Will you come with me whether or not I kill him?"

"Yes, but please don't kill him."

"Why not? It looked to me as if he and this other fool were hurting you when I came."

"Misunderstanding," croaked Kevin, and Drago, seeing his terror, gave a contemptuous smile and began to lower his sword. At which Steve launched himself at his back.

Drago kicked out behind and there was a horrible sound of crunching bone. Steve screamed and dropped under Drago's left elbow. At the same time, Drago's right hand crashed into Kevin's jaw, sending him flying across the floor into a crumpled heap under a bookcase.

Lady Hay screamed. Steve and Kevin moaned. Esther, stunned by the sudden violence, lifted her sickened gaze from Kevin to Drago. He looked savage and ready for more.

"Well?" he demanded. "Do we need anything else?"

Esther swallowed. "My ring."

She turned and went to Kevin. He was out cold. She didn't know if his jaw was broken. In fact, his behaviour today had been so despicable that she didn't greatly care. Instead, she drew the cheque from his pocket and walked back to Lady Hay, who already held out the ring in trembling fingers.

She and Sir Ian stood very close together now. She whispered shakily, "How did he...?"

Sir Ian interrupted. "This is amazing. Truly amazing... Is it Fortune's work?"

"I think so."

"How?"

"I'm not sure. I think that Neturof, the Russian doctor who visited Margaret, used Fortune's magic to discover or perhaps *create* a sort of new dimension from her book, peopled with

Fortune's captured souls—souls waiting to be born, or re-born maybe, or just souls in other dimensions. And managed to send her there, with Fortune's ring. Somehow Fortune is there, too, though what happened to Neturof..."

Drago said, "Neturof *is* Fortune."

"What?" They both stared at Drago, who was gazing down in fascination at the printed pages of *The Prince of Costanzo*. He glanced up.

"It's an anagram."

Esther closed her mouth. Why had she never seen that? Never even looked for it?

Drago said, "Fortune delved deep into the dark magic of many peoples. He told me this when I was a boy. He was determined never to die, and for a long time, with the aid of this ring, he didn't. But internally he was growing weaker and weaker—until he found a way to exist in my world. Through this book, it seems. And so acquired another lifetime."

"And your world?" Hay asked, fascinated. "How can it be created from a book? Do you just live the story? What happens after the story ends?"

"It's not the story," Esther said with certainty. "The setting is the same, and the characters have many of the same names, but they behave differently. It's not history, either. Costanzo never existed in our world, and though it vaguely resembles Renaissance Italy, it just—isn't. And the passage of time in each world isn't related either."

She took a deep breath. "I think—I think Fortune learned how to capture dormant souls by means of his enchanted ring...and finally found a place to put them in Margaret's book."

She spoke to Drago now, seeking his approval, his acceptance of her theory which would surely seem ridiculous to anyone else. "What if the power of our imagination, of our

179

writing, actually creates real dimensions which normally we never know anything about? And which exist entirely in their own time frame, where what *we* understand as past, present and future makes no sense. Their own history and future is extrapolated from the story. Meanwhile, thousands more dimensions are continually created from the imaginations of the peoples of those dimensions. A truly infinite universe..."

No one laughed. Drago's eyes were steadily on hers. "And Fortune's magic got both of them into my—dimension? How?"

"Perhaps, as Neturof, he was with her when she wrote it; perhaps they read it together. Certainly, I'm sure she met him in social circles before she became his patient."

"And by the time they came, my world had always existed... I can live with that. Though I don't care for the idea of being Fortune's captured soul."

Esther frowned. "I'm not sure that you are. He may have captured some which he transferred to your world with him, I don't know. Chiefly, I think, he'd captured his own soul. And Margaret's. And when Margaret's life became unbearable at home, she simply vanished into your world with him. But the souls go their own way. The world grew out of imagination, but the people don't behave as Margaret intended, any more than they do Fortune's bidding now. What they created is far more than either of them."

Hay closed his mouth with a snap. "And the book itself?" He gazed at it with renewed awe. "What *is* it, exactly?"

Drago said slowly, "The book is the passage, the gateway, and also...the means, I think, by which people perceive my world. And I perceive yours. Language for example. You speak English, I hear Italian. Neither of us in each other's worlds will understand words unknown to Margaret. Even Fortune needed it at first—as a sort of binding, I think, to enable him to stay.

Otherwise he would have been drawn back again."

"But losing connection to the book—or the ring—pulls Esther back out."

"I think—as the connection to my world grows—it becomes impossible to go back. Like Margaret."

Esther frowned. "She said she had become *part* of the world and didn't need the ring. Does this mean eventually I won't either?"

"Yes. I had hoped you already were."

There was a lot to take in here. To save herself from drowning in it, she followed one thread determinedly. "Which is why you made no effort to get my ring back from Margaret?"

"Well, that and the fact that taking the ring in my world has no effect on the ring in yours. Besides, she didn't take your ring. It simply stayed here. It was her own ring she gave to you after poisoning my wine."

Esther slapped the heel of her hand to her head. "There are two rings! One in each world! Of course there are. My clothes don't come with me anymore; why should the ring?"

"You are creating your own place in my world, just by being there, drinking the water, eating the food, wearing the clothes, reading the books, interacting with the people. It is not really given for us to inhabit more than one world—dimension, I like that word better—so you must make a choice before it is made for you."

Fascinated, the Hays were looking from one to the other as they spoke. How weird, Esther thought, to be having this conversation here... And yet she couldn't leave it at this turning point. This time, it had to go to the end.

She said, "Your dimension or mine... Can you live in mine?"

Drago looked down at himself, spread his hands. "Apparently. Though under the same laws as you live in mine." He looked around the library to the window, a smile beginning to form on his full, sensual lips. Lips which she suddenly wanted to feel on her again. Could she live here without him now? "It would be fun to see your world..."

Esther smiled. "Come, then..."

His gaze came back to her, the smile dying in his eyes, leaving them serious and rueful. "I can't. I don't know how long I've been away from Costanzo. I have a battle to fight with Fortune and Cosimo."

"A battle?" Esther pounced, startled. "I thought you were simply taking Margaret—"

"Nothing is simple," he interrupted. "Shall we go?"

Esther dragged her gaze free. What was she giving up here? Friends she no longer saw, a sister who'd stopped speaking to her, Kevin whom she'd just ditched and who was staring at her now from the corner, clutching his jaw. A job which bored her. An ambition to write well enough to publish a bestseller... Inconveniently, an idea began to form, was brushed aside for later by the images of the two people she had been trying not to think about, the ones which made the decision less than clear-cut.

"My parents," she whispered. "If I never come back, I won't see them, they'll never know..."

He moved toward her, but not to seize, to force as Kevin had. His hand came up, his long, tapering fingers brushed aside the tear trickling down her cheek.

"It is a hard decision to make. I would like the adventure of knowing your world as well as showing you mine. But I don't think it's possible. We must choose one. And I can't leave Costanzo to Cosimo, can I?"

"No. No you can't."

"You need time to decide what it is you want to do..."

"I know what I *want* to do. But my parents...we're not part of each others' lives much anymore and they're pretty vague anyway. But they *love* me."

"And you love them."

She nodded, hastily wiping her eyes. Her fingers encountered his, became entwined. She pulled his hand to her lips and kissed it.

He said, "I want to give you time, tell you to go and see them, tie up your loose ends and come to me when you're ready. But I don't think you have that option, unless this man will give you the book."

Christ, she had forgotten about the Hays, still avidly drinking in their little tragedy. Hay looked alarmed, his gaze swinging to the book as if he wished he were between it and them.

"I don't think he'll do that," Esther said sardonically.

"He won't," Hay agreed. "But he would give you access to it. Through fascination rather than softness of heart, I might add."

"Whenever I wanted?" Esther pounced.

"If we're here."

Esther, prickling with conflicting doubts and hopes, glanced at Lady Hay.

Drago said what they were all thinking. "Do you trust them?"

And the truth was, no she didn't. They had both been prepared to conspire with Kevin to obtain the ring, for different reasons. Hay might be fascinated by their story, but there were any number of reasons why he might deny her the book.

She glanced back at Drago, indecision tearing her apart.

"There may be another way," he said reluctantly. "I *might* be able to bring you back. Maybe just once, maybe a few times. Maybe not. No guarantees, but I will try."

Her heart lifted and soared. Perhaps it was foolish, but her decision was made. She flung both arms around his neck, and he hugged her hard.

But suddenly she was thinking of practicalities. Like Margaret, she had to make arrangements. Over Drago's shoulder she met Hay's still ultra-curious gaze.

"One thing... You're not going to want a comatose body lying around your library indefinitely. If I can come back, I'll fix that. But..." Slipping out of Drago's arms, she reached for her notepad and pen, scribbling down a phone number. "If I'm not here by tomorrow morning, phone my sister and she'll take me away."

"One other thing," Drago added. "Please leave the ring on her finger."

Considering how much it had once meant to her, it was odd how little she seemed to value it now. "But travelling with you, I won't need it, will I?"

"If we want to get back, we'll need all the connections we can muster," Drago said with a trace of grimness." His eyes were not on hers but on Hay's. Sir Ian was smiling, and yet behind the easy acceptance was pure speculation.

Trust? Jesus, no farther than I could throw him! This isn't safe...

Drago said softly, "I can find you anywhere."

And Hay's gaze fell abruptly. "As I already explained, I am happy to be your host for the sake of curiosity. Threats are unnecessary."

"What a joy to meet a man of honour. Esther."

Without hesitation, she took his outstretched hand. From the corner of her eye, she could see Kevin and Steve, sitting up now, open-mouthed and staring.

"How *did* you get here?" Sir Ian demanded, suddenly urgent.

Drago regarded him over her head. She felt rather than saw him smile. "It says in your book—I'm a sorcerer."

Laughter caught in Esther's throat as the world began to swing. She started to say, "And an evil usurper..." But already the world swung, spinning down into darkness, dragging her on a different journey.

She knew an instant of fear that he had taken the wrong road for it felt like a new one to her, and then abruptly, the light was back. There was birdsong in her ears, and sweet, earthy forest scents in her nostrils. The weight of a man on her body, between her legs, deep inside her.

Chapter Thirteen

She gasped, her body jerking involuntarily to free itself. She grasped the hair of the head so close to hers and wrenched it back.

Drago's eyes were closed and there was a smile on his face.

"I love it when you're rough." His eyes opened. Pushing against her grip, he lowered his head inexorably to hers and began to kiss her mouth. At the same time, he moved inside her, a tender, exploratory motion that sent immediate shock waves through every nerve of her body. It was delicious.

Esther surrendered, giving herself up to the kiss, arching her hips into his and moaning as he drew himself out almost all the way and then slid back in. She had wakened wet, so there was no discomfort, just sudden, galloping need and pleasure so great she thought she would die of it before they finished.

But Drago wouldn't let her quicken his leisurely pace. Smiling into her mouth, he released it long enough to say, "There's no hurry."

Only when he pushed his hands between them to unbuckle his sword-belt, did she register that while she was naked, he was fully dressed, an inconvenience she helped him deal with quite urgently. Every movement sent sparks of intense pleasure through her.

"No hurry," he repeated teasingly, using his feet to push off his leggings.

"I thought you had to fight Fortune and Cosimo." She gasped as he brushed his lips across her naked breast and flicked his tongue around her nipple.

"We have two hours until midday. With the best will in the world, he can't get here before then. And besides, I'll hear him coming."

"You're scary," she whispered, running her hands down his newly naked back, caressing the rippling muscles and clearly defined vertebrae, sweeping them over the curve of his taut buttocks so that she could press him closer inside her.

They appeared to be in a tent, lying on a bedroll on the ground. Around them, mercifully outside the tent, she could hear not-so-distant voices, talking, laughing, the snort of horses, the trampling of hooves and human feet on the ground.

Drago pushed inside her with an incredibly sensual circular motion that ignited more pleasure points than she'd been aware she had, and she clung to him with her internal muscles, hugging and caressing his cock as he moved it inside her.

"You're beautiful," he returned. "These are beautiful." And he took her breast into his mouth and began to suck strongly. The bliss began to build faster.

"Is that why you brought me with you after all?" she whispered, closing her eyes as delight consumed her body with increasing strength.

"Of course. Once I recovered enough to see that your sleep was the deep one that took you from us, I was afraid to leave you. I needed to be sure you could come back. I was only guessing about the ring, until I saw it for sure in your world."

As he spoke, he increased his pace, thrusting with greater rhythm. Esther, with urgent need to see him, opened her eyes again, felt her pleasure re-double at the hot, clouded passion she read in his eyes. She knew he wanted to slam into her, empty himself inside her in desperate release right now. Yet he controlled the pace to extend the pleasure, to make it all the greater when he let them have it. The effort it cost him made his breath ragged, his arms tremble as he caressed her. Sweat trickled down his forehead, glistened on his upper lip.

"So you brought me here, and then what?" she gasped. "Made love to me while I slept? Christ, how do I feel about that?"

"You didn't seem to mind at the time."

"I was asleep! I wasn't even there!"

He kissed her. "I needed the connection to find you... The universe is vast. Though you'd gone, your body still held enough of your essence to let me follow. I made them all leave me here alone with you, then I undressed you, lay down here with you and pushed my cock inside you, like this..."

Esther moaned as he drove into her, all the way up to his balls.

"Then came the difficult part. Because I had to feel every inch of you and not make love to you. It was hard," he added, moving faster and more forcefully, "but I managed it. And of course it had the added advantage that I could take my pleasure in you as soon as we came back."

"You can't have known," Esther gasped, clinging to him, thrusting and writhing under him as the pleasure rose inexorably higher. It was going to be so huge that she'd die... "Time passes here while you're gone."

"Not necessarily," he ground out, slamming into her. "I'm a sorcerer."

Esther cried out as the waves crashed through her, casting her higher and higher, breaking her helpless body on a relentless rack of pleasure. Convulsing around him, she cried out again as he thrust hard one more time and released his own joy in jet after jet of hot seed, impossibly heightening her delight.

He collapsed on her in glorious abandon, seizing her mouth in a huge kiss that only partly smothered his shouts of pleasure.

Time seemed to stand still as sensation rocked and slowly, gradually, righted them.

"Aren't I?" he whispered breathlessly.

"A sorcerer?" She smiled. "Oh yes."

He laughed softly, shifting his weight and turning her with him so that they could lie side by side without separating. Surrounded by desultory noise and activity, the tent gave the illusion of isolation. But it *was* only an illusion. Esther snuggled closer.

"I suppose we should get up and go out there."

"Why? There's plenty of time."

"Won't they...suspect what we're doing in here?"

Drago grinned. "No, they know damned well what we're doing. Privilege of rank."

"It's good to be the prince," Esther murmured, half-amused, half-appalled by the publicity of their relationship.

"Right now, it's very good," he agreed.

She moved her head, grazing her teeth across his shoulder. "I could make it even better," she offered wickedly.

"Do you know I hoped you would say that?"

Esther bit down gently, then moved to straddle him. It felt amazing to hold this perfect man between her legs, his cock nestling, still hard, among the folds of her pussy, his strong, handsome face alight with lustful anticipation. Smiling with

189

sheer happiness, she lay forward to kiss his chest, flickering her tongue across his stiff nipples, tracing her fingers around the scattering of dark hair on his chest, feeling the scars on his skin as well as the hard muscle beneath and the strong frame of his ribs. She moved lower, dragging a line of kisses to his navel, sliding her body lower down his thigh, while her finger followed the fine, sexy line of hair down his stomach, almost but not quite touching his fully erect, quivering cock.

Slowly, increasing his tension, she lowered her head, watching him all the time as she wrapped first her hand and then her lips around his shaft, licking her way up to the soft, velvety head. His eyes closed. He muttered something below his breath that sounded like, "Thank you, God."

"How long have we got?" she asked, low-voiced.

"Long enough," he said fervently. "Right now, long enough for me is about two minutes, but feel free to experiment."

She did.

ω

Esther finally emerged from the tent some ten minutes after Drago had left. Fortune, he said, was close; he had gone to make sure his men were aware of it.

"Where's Matilda?" she'd asked, dragging herself from her sensual daze back to more mundane matters.

"Under guard."

"Then no one believed her accusation that I'd poisoned you?"

"Hardly. The people in that room were my friends and supporters. And she was the only one who didn't know the significance of the pearls. She might have thought they were a gift to a whore. Everyone else knew they were my mother's, and a marriage gift."

She'd said lightly, "But we're not married."

And from the tent doorway, he'd smiled back at her, shrinking the distance between them. "Father Luca will take care of that. Tonight."

Even remembering the way he'd said "tonight" made her flesh tingle. Well, tingle more. She still felt warm and hazy with the afterglow of the most stupendous sex she'd ever encountered. Drago made love with his whole body, not just his cock, spectacular though that organ was...

Hastily, Esther dragged her thoughts to less inflammatory matters. Fortune was on his way, and although Drago made light of a trap, Esther was sure there would be one of some kind. She wasn't alone in that. However, everyone else just backed down before Drago's impatience. Esther wished Arturo was here, since he alone seemed to be unafraid of the prince.

Drago lounged on a stool by a trestle table, his long legs stretched out before him, crossed at the ankles. A jug and several cups lay on the table, around which several officers sat arguing over a game of dice.

Drago appeared to have lost interest in the game. His eyes were closed and he might have been asleep except that for some reason Esther knew he wasn't. As she made her way toward him, a shout went up, like a signal of some kind. Another shout sounded in return and someone scuttled past her to the prince.

"Sir! Sir! My lord, he's coming!"

"I know," said Drago without opening his eyes. "How many men?"

"About the same as us."

"Excellent." Drago tipped his hat down over his face. The

officer opened his mouth to speak, then closed it again and swallowed his words. As he turned away, he met Esther's gaze and a brief, almost involuntary communication passed between them.

Esther walked faster. "Is it, Drago?" she said, as she approached him. The officer hovered, while the other men at the table all stood courteously.

"Is it what?" Drago asked lazily, pushing his hat up again. "Oh brightest flower in my garden of love."

Esther couldn't help her snort of laughter. "Stop it," she reproved. "I'm serious! Is it really excellent that Fortune's approaching with only as many men as us?"

"Makes for a fairer fight," Drago responded judiciously.

"But Drago, he has many more than that! *Where are the rest of them?*"

Drago opened one eye. "Back at Cosimo's main camp. I've taken every precaution, trust me." On the last two words, he opened his other eye too and looked not at her but at the officer, who bowed, apparently satisfied and walked away.

Drago uncrossed one foot, stretched it under the table and hooked one of the vacated stools, dragging it over beside him. "Take a seat," he invited. "Have some wine and tell me how much you love me. Ignore these brutes," he added amiably as one of his companions sniggered. "Even their mothers don't love them."

"It's as well we've got you then, sir," one of them quipped, and Drago pushed the jug toward him.

"That's what I think."

As Esther looked around her more carefully, she realized that Drago's men were far more prepared than she'd thought at first glance. Many of them stood at ease, but all were armed and alert. Hawk-eyed officers stood at strategic points, watching and waiting, and Esther realized belatedly that the little show of the officers sprawling over their wine and dice was merely a bit of theatre to annoy Fortune.

Apart from the tent she and Drago had just left, there was only one other in the camp. At its doorway now stood Matilda-Margaret, her hand on the canvas, waiting. Two sentries guarded her, two more at the back of the tent.

In front of the camp, stood the small village of Monteverini, sprawling down the hill. Behind it, majestic green mountains rose, a magnificent background to whatever would unfold here this afternoon.

John Fortune rode up the hill from the village at a gallop, his men streaming out behind him. Encountering Drago's men, suddenly at attention and in formation only yards away, they reined in.

As one, the men at Esther's table stood and made their way toward their own men. Fortune, perhaps catching the movement, perhaps seeing him all along, gazed directly at Drago while his horse plunged its head and snorted.

Drago waved. Negligently, he unwound his legs and stood. "Come with me if you want to," he said casually to Esther, who had every intention of doing so anyhow. "But Esther?"

"What?" She hurried beside him as he strolled across the ground.

"Stay behind me. Don't ever get between him and me."

Her stomach twisted as she absorbed this terse instruction. Unlike anything else he had said to her since they'd come out of the tent, this time he was serious.

The men had formed in front of Matilda's tent, blocking the lady from Fortune's view. But if Matilda could really communicate with him telepathically, presumably he knew where she was anyhow. It was Drago who held his attention, Drago and Esther as they picked their way across the rough, dry ground under the glare of the midday sun.

They walked in front of the soldiers, Esther farthest from Fortune and his men, until they stood at the centre of the front line, facing Fortune. Obedient to her instructions, Esther stepped back a pace. Fortune's eyes, narrowed against the sun, raked her quickly, almost avidly, then returned to Drago. He had not dismounted, and being able to look down on his enemy should have given him dominance of the scene, yet somehow it didn't. Drago possessed in abundance the sort of charismatic presence politicians only dreamed of.

"*Mister* Fortune," said Drago.

"Sir," returned Fortune, clearly determined not to use his title. "How is my wife?"

"She is well." Drago raised his hand commandingly, and two soldiers began to come forward with Matilda walking between them, head held high. Again Fortune's gaze flickered to Esther

"And her kinswoman, the lady Esther?"

"Also well, as you see."

In the short silence, Fortune's gaze moved around the field, taking in the positions and numbers of Drago's men. "I asked, if you recall, that she also be returned to us."

"I recall it perfectly. I choose not to comply."

"Why not? You want another hostage?"

"*Another* hostage? My sister was hardly a hostage. She came of her own free will and without invitation. Between you and me she's not much of a peace negotiator either, but I enjoyed having her." Drago smiled serenely at his old tutor, whose eyes narrowed at this no doubt deliberate ambiguity. So did Esther's. Jealousy twisted inside her, just because Drago *might* have...

Matilda, who was now close enough to hear, gave a tinkling laugh as she approached. "Be careful how you phrase things, sir. My husband is a jealous man."

"Are you?" Drago asked with interest. "Well, you've no need to be. I return my sister to you without regret." He smiled once more. "I tired of her."

"He's trying to rile you, John," Matilda said quickly as her husband's hands jerked involuntarily on the reins, causing his horse to sidestep. "Of course he never touched me, and nor would I let him. He is my brother."

"Though no blood relation. And I am, of course, evil," Drago pointed out. He gazed up at the rigid figure of his enemy. "Or so people say. Did you want something else?"

"My wife's kinswoman," Fortune said stiffly.

"I haven't tired of *her*."

"He has made her his whore," Matilda mourned.

"And you," Drago said to her, "are not invited to the wedding."

"*Wedding?*" Fortune looked genuinely startled this time. Matilda's mouth fell open. "Is this another of your poor-taste jokes?"

"I only joke with friends."

The eyes of the two men locked. Something almost tangible passed between them, as if even now Fortune was trying to reestablish his authority over his wayward pupil. The air seemed to crackle with some silent battle. And yet neither of them moved.

At last, Fortune laughed. It wasn't a pleasant sound. "It will do you no good, you know. You'll get no heir on her. Coming here makes them barren."

Startled, Esther's gaze flew to Drago. It was something she'd never even thought of. Marriage was outrageous enough; babies and heirs were way beyond her mind's ability to contemplate right now. But princes, rulers, always needed heirs...Was it true?

Drago's profile gave nothing away. He didn't even glance at her. He said mildly, "Well, then you can relax and just wait for Cosimo to succeed me."

Then would all his struggles not be for nothing if he simply handed the country over to his cousin in the end anyway?

"What will you do?" Fortune sneered. "Sire a brat on a mistress and pass it off as your wife's? Pass Costanzo from one bastard to another?"

Once, Esther thought, it would have hurt him. It would have hurt the boy she had first seen crying in his bedroom over his father's rejection and humiliation. Drago didn't smile now, but nor did he show any signs of tension or anger.

"It depends on your definition of bastard. As for whom I sleep with, if you want a list, you'll need to apply to my secretary in writing."

The pain never really got started. With something approaching wonder, Esther realized that the joke was for her, a perverse reassurance of his faithfulness. *"I only joke with friends."*

"And now that we understand each other all over again and your wife is safely delivered, do you have anything for me? Submission, perhaps? I can be clement, you know—can't I, Alessandro?"

Previously unnoticed. Alessandro de Verini edged his horse a little closer and bowed. Fortune stared at him. Irritation sparked in his eyes, a little spite perhaps, but no real malevolence. Which alarmed Esther. It was almost as if Fortune didn't really care about this not inconsiderable blow. Why should that be, unless...unless he believed he had already won?

Shit!

"Traitor," Fortune pronounced with contempt.

"On the contrary, though I have been so, I have now returned to the allegiance I should never have left. You lied to me. It is you and Cosimo who are the traitors, you and Cosimo who are ruining this country. I stand with Prince Drago, who is great enough to forgive my stupidity."

It won a cheer from Drago's men, and from the local folk— Alessandro's own—who were still gathering to watch this apparently peaceful spectacle.

This time Fortune didn't even look annoyed. He merely shrugged it off, waited for the noise to die down before he again addressed Drago.

"Since we are here, and since my wife has had no success promoting peace between us, perhaps you and I could achieve more face to face."

"Now? You want to talk about peace? Sure." Drago waved one hand expansively behind him to the camp they had set up. "Be my guest."

"You expect me to come alone into your camp?"

"You can bring one companion. Your men, I regret, must stay where they are."

"Or we could talk here."

"Are you trying to swelter or bore our armies to death?" Drago enquired.

"Let's see if we can't make it interesting for everyone."

"I can't help but admire an optimist. Let's have a table and chairs here. And wine, of course. She," he added, pointing at a suddenly frightened Matilda, "does not come near the wine."

It was weird, almost surreal. Fortune, with another man she recognized from her brief stay in Cosimo's camp, sat down at the table with Drago and herself and Father Luca, who materialized as if from nowhere. Wine was poured, though little was drunk. And the men talked, although little was said.

It came to Esther that they were waiting for something. Both of them. With dread, she constantly scoured the horizon, listened for the sounds of approaching horses or marching men, for any cries or sounds that might denote attack. Drago was too sure of himself, too carelessly arrogant... He believed he could defeat Fortune, could adapt to whatever was thrown at him. Perhaps he could, but Esther feared the slaughter that would come with it, wished he did, too...

She found herself watching the men. Fortune's mounted soldiers stayed alert. Drago's, though physically at ease, looked distinctly *un*easy. Alessandro gazed toward the mountain, to the higher foothills as if, like her, he, too, could imagine the sounds of approaching soldiers, even see them moving through the vines and trees like columns of fast-moving, single-minded ants...

"My lord," Alessandro said quietly, and Esther's heart leapt into her throat. *Real. Jesus, they really are soldiers...*

Drago glanced up at him. "I know." He had heard them long ago. Cosimo had told her at the very beginning about his hearing, magically enhanced... Why was he just sitting there? There would have been time to escape if they'd gone earlier.

Fortune sat back in his seat. "It's over, Drago. Surrender now and save us all the hell of more bloodshed."

"Why would I do that?" Drago asked. He sounded genuinely curious.

"Cosimo is coming. If you cannot sense him, I can."

"I sense him."

"He's bringing the rest of our army. You are surrounded, Drago. Yield."

Drago twisted around to gaze at the speedily growing columns galloping down from the hills. "That's a lot of men," he observed. "How much does it cost to pay so many mercenaries?"

"It costs *you* Costanzo. Shortly after I set out, so did Cosimo, with the rest of our army. You were listening for *me* by then and didn't hear him. He's taken the route across the hills and trapped you."

Drago reached for his wine, pushing his seat around for a better look at the approaching army. Esther could make out the individual shapes now. The noise was getting louder, a triumphant army on the move. Drago gave no orders, though every man in the camp gazed at him, waiting. It seemed he accepted the truth and would not fight. What did that mean? *Would they kill him? Oh Jesus...*

But curiously, Drago's calm remained intact. For some reason that soothed her. It seemed to soothe all of them. Perhaps that was magic, too...

Drago said conversationally, "Before you set out—before any of us set out—my friend Arturo left my castle. *You* were listening for *me* and did not hear him. He has taken your camp, defeated your mercenaries and taken Cosimo and any other live Costanzans prisoner. I'm afraid it's you who are trapped, *Mister* Fortune."

Esther couldn't help it. She laughed. It was relief and admiration and fury at being kept in the dark, all rolled into one. The sheer strength of the emotion had to get out somehow.

Drago glanced at her and winked. And with a roar, Fortune leapt to his feet, knocking over the table as he went. Esther jumped aside as jug and cups went flying, splashing wine liberally around people and ground. Fortune launched himself across the upended table directly at Drago, who alone had remained sitting. But there was a dagger in Fortune's hand, and before Esther could scream, before she or the others had begun to throw themselves at Drago's killer, she already knew it would be too late. His arm had swung back as he leapt; there was force enough surely to kill...

Grief and fury roared through her, and stopped dead like the point of Fortune's dagger, which slammed to a halt less than an inch from Drago's heart.

On her knees at Drago's side, Esther stared in weird fascination at the trembling dagger point, at Fortune's effort-contorted face as he tried and failed to push it home. Luca and Alessandro, poised one on either side of Fortune to pull him off, froze, staring like everyone else at the dagger.

A groan of rage and exhaustion escaped Fortune. His eyes lifted with hatred to Drago's.

Drago, unmoving, said, "You always taught me that anger was the worst enemy of the sorcerer."

The dagger began to move, not on to Drago's heart, but turned, slowly, until it pointed instead at Fortune. Mesmerized, everyone stared at it.

With a grunt of effort, Fortune opened his fist, but the released dagger did not fall. It hung in the air like a phantom.

"Dear God, Drago," Father Luca whispered, crossing himself.

But Drago never took his gaze off Fortune.

The Englishman forced a smile. "It seems you learned the lesson better than I had ever imagined. While I forgot it. Anger, uncontrolled emotion, was always *your* weakness."

"Not any more. My anger, like my revenge, is cold. So cold

it's icy."

"Revenge for what, Drago? Supporting the other side? Choosing Cosimo rather than you?"

Sweat broke out on Drago's brow. "I forgive you that, John. I wouldn't have been any sort of tool for you. What I *don't* forgive is your harrying of my people. And I don't forgive you the murder of my father."

The knife drove straight and true for Fortune's heart. Letting out a cry of pure fear, he tried to grab it, and found his hand up against some immovable force. He couldn't get his fingers near enough to seize it. He scrabbled backwards, his legs scuttling like a crab, his backside dragging through the dusty ground.

"Drago stop it, you can't kill me. You mustn't! For Christ's sake I did you a favour. *He betrayed you.*"

Drago smiled at the hysteria in his old tutor's voice. "I *can* kill you, of course. Legally, too. To be honest, I don't much care whether I do or not. A confession might make me feel more lenient..."

"Christ, I confess, I confess!"

"Confess to what?"

"To killing him," Fortune screamed, as the dagger poked into his throat. Again he scrabbled back and the dagger followed as though attached to his skin. "I poisoned Rudolfo to clear Cosimo's way. And I poisoned his wife to ensure no other awkward heirs. For Christ's sake, call it off, Drago!"

"You're the sorcerer," said Drago contemptuously. "You call it off."

And standing up with incomparable grace, he simply turned and walked away.

Esther, her gaze still clinging to Fortune with mingled

satisfaction and pity, scrambled after Drago.

"What will...?" She broke off, for Drago's face was wet with tears.

Wordlessly, she slid her hand into his and, without slowing his stride, he gripped it convulsively.

"Drago," Fortune screamed behind them. He had backed into his men, who were shifting restlessly, beginning to disperse to escape Arturo's approaching army. When he seized someone's foot to help him rise, the soldier kicked him contemptuously and rode off. And the knife still clung to Fortune's throat.

Alessandro and Luca moved after him, and in total terror now, he latched onto the priest. "Help me, help me," he gibbered.

"I cannot help you, my son. You've lived too long, and yet you want to live forever. Well, not here, not any more. Not in our country."

Fortune turned and fled as though all the fiends in hell were after him. The dagger followed, whizzing and whirling with his every movement.

"This time," said Luca clearly, "it really is over."

ω

"But it isn't, is it?" said Esther as she and Drago and their escort watched the two lonely figures ride across the border and into exile once more. Cosimo and Matilda-Margaret. The wooded hills dwarfed them, swallowed them. "They'll find Fortune and keep coming back, because this place is what draws Fortune. The book binds him, too."

"I believe so. He'll have figured out how to call the dagger off, when he calmed down. He'll remember the fear and humiliation for a while, but he cannot live any longer as 'an ordinary man'. He has to be the power behind the throne or it isn't worth it for him now. He will try again to bring Cosimo back."

"What will you do? Can magic keep him out?"

"For a time, perhaps for longer than last time. But sooner or later, he'll break down my spells."

Drago pulled on the reins, dragging his horse around so that instead he looked over Costanzo, the picturesque villages scattered among rolling valleys and vine-laden hills. In the distance, a castle, perhaps Drago's own.

Abruptly, he said, "I don't want my people suffering this every few years. Worse, one day he might even defeat me."

Esther edged her own horse closer to his, so that she could touch his hand. It turned, dropping the reins to grip hers. He smiled at her. "When was the last time I made love to you?"

"This morning," said Esther, flushing all over at the memory. He had some wonderful techniques in oral sex... With an effort, she brought her wayward mind back to serious matters. She was not after all, a mere sex object. She didn't mind the sex, but the mere was out.

She said, "Could this work?" And told him about the idea that had come to her in the Hays' library. Drago began to laugh.

Chapter Fourteen

Esther sat in her parents' kitchen, drinking coffee with them. From the window, she could see Drago, looking damned sexy in hip-hugging jeans and a t-shirt, investigating with deep interest the engine of her father's car.

"Does he know what he's doing?" her mother asked with vague unease.

"Hasn't a clue," Esther confessed. "He's just trying to see how it works; he won't *damage* it."

"I'll get him one of those DIY car mechanic books for Christmas," said her father comfortably.

Esther smiled. They had taken to Drago surprisingly well. Kevin they had merely tolerated in their vague, unassuming way. "You like him then?"

"He's a bit strange," her mother observed. "But he has a nice smile. And I've never seen you look so happy."

Esther blinked, gazing at her mother's amiable, generally distracted countenance. She hadn't been aware that either of them noticed her happiness. Or otherwise.

"I'm going back to Italy with him," she said.

"That'll be nice," said her father approvingly. "Beautiful country. Charming people."

"Yes...but I might not be able to get back as often as I'd

like."

"Just send us a postcard occasionally so we know you're all right."

A postcard. In the age of computers and mobile phones there was really no excuse for the occasional postcard. Esther bit her lip. She should be grateful for their immunity to modern technology. And at least her sister Jenny lived close by...

Delving into her pocket, she brought out a pendant. It had been made in Costanzo, deliberately lower-key than Drago's affronted jeweller had designed in twenty years. Yet even so, its beauty was eye-catching. A simple peridot in a plain gold setting, hung on a thick golden chain.

"We brought you this," Esther said, giving it to her mother. "I thought you'd like it."

Please don't lose it, or be burgled! But if you do there's always this...

And she handed her father a small stone carving of a wolf. Drago had made it, as he had made the statue of the woman in his bedroom—another unexpected talent. "It would look well in your study," she said with forced lightness.

As her parents gazed in surprised awe at their unexpected gifts, she added awkwardly, "If you need me, touch them. Who knows? I might feel it."

They looked at her. Her father said, "Is something going on, Esther?"

Esther shook her head, felt like crying. Fortunately, the kitchen door opened and Drago came in.

Her mother said, "Where's your Gran's ring?"

"I left it with Jenny. She's looking after it for me."

Jenny had been so surprised by her visit that she'd forgotten to sulk. Instead, she'd cheered over Kevin's downfall and demanded to meet the new man. Well, maybe one day...

Three objects, two of them made by their own hands—the pendant under careful, outraged instruction—and enchanted by Drago, connecting Costanzo to her old life. Since as yet he had so small a connection to this dimension, he had been able to bring them with him. He doubted he'd be able to do so again. She hoped it would be enough to let them come back. Just sometimes. Because she suspected their welcome at the Hays' was officially worn out. They'd broken a glass cabinet emerging from the book this morning and scared the wits out of both Lady Hay and the housekeeper. In fact, the two women had turned so nasty that Drago had resorted to haughty prince mode and stared them down with disdain as he'd stepped over the carnage with Esther on his arm and walked straight out of the house without a backward glance.

Esther still thought it was funny.

Drago lowered his long, lean body onto the chair beside her and nudged her with his elbow, a gesture of comfort as well as a reminder.

"Are you ready to go?"

"Yes, of course."

"Flight to catch?" asked her mother brightly. "Do you want sandwiches?"

Laughter that was close to tears caught in Esther's throat. "No thanks, Mum, we'll be fine. Oh, and I heard today there's an agent interested in the book I wrote about Margaret Marsden. She thinks she knows exactly the publisher for it—it looks really promising."

Esther had come alone a month ago with her completed manuscript. She hadn't expected the first agent she'd tried to grab it.

"Wonderful news," beamed her father. Publishing books

was something he could understand, even if fiction was hardly his cup of tea. The novel had turned into a unique mixture of history and dark fantasy that had blown the agent away.

"Now you'll have to write another," said her mother.

"I already have," Esther said lightly. Although it wouldn't ever see the light of day in this dimension. "Anyway, while I'm away, Jenny will take care of legal stuff and royalties. And you'll get a free book." She stood. So did Drago, who amazed and rather delighted her mother by kissing her on both cheeks. Her father, looking rather more alarmed, received much the same treatment, and then Drago strode to the door while she made her own goodbyes.

"Drago," her father murmured, adding obscurely, "I always thought you were a bit of a dragon type." He smiled in his vague gentle way and opened the door.

ω

"What if they *still* come back?" she asked, curling into Drago's naked body. They were staying in the house of a minor local landowner, who had been delighted to give up his bed chamber to the prince, especially when told their visit was secret and important state business.

Wide awake, Esther looked forward eagerly to the sort of distractions her husband usually offered. On the other hand, doubts about tomorrow still niggled her, and Drago seemed more inclined to fall asleep than to make love to her.

Piqued, she slid her hand over the hard curve of his hip and down his lean, muscled thigh which moved under her touch in instant response.

He said, "There's nothing to bind them here. It's possible

Fortune could find a way, but why should he? You've written him a perfect world. He can be king and Cosimo can betray him for a change. If it stays the same as you wrote it. Which it probably won't since the souls will go their own way."

"That's another thing. I feel sorry for the souls we're giving them charge of. It's not really very ethical, is it? Save ourselves and our own people at the expense of the unknown souls we sacrificed. It's like playing God. Or the Devil."

His hand covered hers as it quested upwards to his taut stomach. Grasping it, he pulled it to his cock and pressed it there. She laughed breathlessly into his shoulder.

"I'm trying to be serious, Drago."

"No you're not. You're trying to tease me. We've talked about it before. We can't control the growth or the experience of souls, and who knows, in the right environment, maybe even Fortune's will grow. And Matilda's. Cosimo will always be paltry." He glanced down to where her hand wrapped around his cock. "Are you going to do anything with that, or just hold it?"

"Just hold it for a bit."

"Then let me hold something of yours." He rolled over, grasping her between the legs so firmly that she gasped.

Releasing his cock to wind her arms around him instead, she whispered, "Drago? Will you mind if I can't have children?"

She hadn't meant to say it, and God knew it was the worst time to bring up such a thing. But Drago didn't bat an eyelid.

"Will *you*?" he asked, moving his hand sensuously. He began to trace kisses down her throat, seeking the place on her nape that drove her wild.

"Would you really take a mistress in order to have an heir?"

"Only if she was beautiful and willing. And only if you let

me. And watched," he added, as though much struck. "Do you think it would be fun?"

"I don't want to share you," she whispered. "I love you."

He paused, lifting his head to look down at her. Slowly, he began to smile. "Good."

He moved his body over hers, nudged his cock between her legs. Her hands dug into his shoulders, pleading. "What?" Gazing into her eyes, he pushed his cock inside her, groaning softly with pleasure as he went. "Do you really need to hear me say that I've loved you since I first saw you ten years ago?"

"That wasn't love. You didn't know me."

"Yes I did, but I know you better, and love you better now."

She buried her face in his neck. She felt his hand cradling her head, heard him murmur with wonder, "You really didn't know, did you?" And he pushed into her, slowly, achingly. The pleasure was intense, enabling her to swallow the foolish tears, to find a better outlet for her emotion.

"I still don't," she challenged, arching up into him. "You'll have to show me."

"With pleasure," he returned.

"There had better be," she gasped out.

ω

They had stayed in this inn before. Nestling in the hills which bordered Costanzo, it had housed them on their wedding night. After Fortune had fled from the dagger and they had sent Matilda and Cosimo back into exile.

Despite what they had come here to do, Esther found her mind and body melting at the intrusive memory. Drago had not let her close her eyes all night, insisting they look at each other through every moment of loving, whether tender, passionate or fierce. And he had been all three and more as he'd ravished her through that night. Turned into pure lust herself, a barely thinking collection of sensual pleasure points, she rather thought she had been, too. She couldn't get enough of him, his athletic, sensual body, his wild, arousing lips, those clever, tender hands with their long, too-sensitive fingers, and his big, enduring cock eternally thrusting inside her, seeking her pussy or her mouth with equal urgency.

Now, with the brief flash of memory, a flood of moisture pooled between her thighs. Later, perhaps, they could repeat it...

But now, she had to keep her wits about her, or they were both dead.

The inn's main room was dim, but merry enough, full of local men and a couple of chickens clucking about their feet. Apart from the odd casual glance, no one paid Esther or Drago much attention. They were incognito.

The innkeeper himself bustled to meet them, bowing low. "I am busy tonight, my lord, but I can offer you and your lady a most pleasant room..."

"We'll decide that later," Drago interrupted. Muffled against the winter cold of the mountains, his face was barely visible between his fur-lined cloak and his hat. Striding across the hall with Esther at his heels, he reached for the parlour door.

"No, no," protested the agitated innkeeper. "My lord, that room is already taken."

"I know," said Drago and went in.

At the table in the centre of the room sat three men and a woman. John Fortune glanced up at the opening door and smiled without surprise. If he remembered the humiliation of his last encounter with Drago, no one could tell.

"Drago," he said blandly. "How nice of you to join us. And you brought your lady wife? How pleasant."

His manner didn't change, and yet Esther had the feeling that her presence was not expected. He had "heard" Drago, but not her. Cosimo had leapt to his feet, was reaching for his sword.

"Now now, my prince," Fortune chided, catching his arm. "Your cousin is our guest. I presume, since his army is not with him, that he has not come to force us back into exile with any more of his little toys."

"What would be the point?" Drago said, swinging off his cloak and hat, chivalrously taking Esther's. "You keep coming back."

"True. And your protection spells seem to be losing their strength. It took me years last time. This time, barely six months."

"Perhaps you're getting better at unravelling them," said Drago, knowing full well he had done the majority of the unravelling himself. He wanted this finished.

"Please, sit down, join us. A cup of wine?"

"No, thank you," said Drago, looking pointedly at Matilda, who laughed. Drago smiled, a smile that grew to encompass all of them, Fortune, Cosimo, and the unknown youth who half-stood, half-sat nervously plucking at his tunic. Another noble landowner, recently come of age. Another tool for Fortune, like Alessandro.

"I have come," said Drago, "to offer you peace."

"Peace," Fortune repeated sardonically.

"On what terms?" sneered Cosimo. The family resemblance between Drago and him was strong, and yet what Esther had once taken for gentleness in his face—at least when compared with Drago's—she now saw was weakness. Fortune had a perfect puppet. "Of bowing to you and swearing allegiance?"

"That's it," said Drago, looking pleased. "Do it now and I won't stand in your way of coming home."

Cosimo blinked. "You won't?"

"Of course not. I am a calmer man. I have found inner peace."

"Through your new 'princess'?" Matilda asked incredulously. Her inverted commas around the title were both palpable and insulting, but Drago appeared not to notice.

"Indeed," he said, bowing in Esther's direction. "But more than that, I have found God."

The unknown youth stared at him. "You have renounced the Devil?"

"Oh for God's sake," Esther muttered in irritation at Fortune's continuing propaganda. Fortune smiled at her tauntingly, but again Drago let it pass.

He said seriously, "Entirely. Father Luca and I have talked much over the last few months and I now realize what has been lacking in the whole country as well as in my own life." He beamed around the room, while Esther looked away as though embarrassed. "Forgiveness."

Fortune's eyes flickered to her, then back to Drago. "*Now* you want to forgive us?"

"Exactly."

"Even for harrying 'your' people and murdering your father?"

Drago's face never twitched. "Well, if your wife can forgive you for murdering her mother, I'm sure I can be as large-hearted."

The difference was, of course, that Margaret had never regarded Matilda's mother as her own. She was just a woman in the "play" she had found so much more interesting than her constricting real life.

"And what then?" Fortune asked. "You'll trust us to come to court and be good?"

"If you swear to be. On the Bible."

Fortune sat back in his seat, staring at Drago's gently smiling face. "I almost believe you. What do you think of this—er—plan, my lady?"

Esther glanced at him, then quickly away, avoiding Drago's gaze, too. "I don't trust you at all," she muttered. "Any of you. However, I'm prepared to believe that an oath sworn on the Bible means more in this world than it does in mine."

"Even for me? Don't you know what I was?"

"I read your book. You never denied God, merely looked beyond the teachings of the Church."

Fortune smiled slightly, glanced at Cosimo, who laughed.

"You know, I think my cousin has found a new enthusiasm. A reformed prince! Have you considered the cloister, Drago?"

"I *have* considered it," Drago said seriously. "Perhaps in the future...but for now, you must swear your sincere oaths of allegiance on the Bible and I will let you come to court unhindered." His lip curled. "Without men-at-arms, of course. Minimal escort. I'm not completely trusting."

That was a nice touch, Esther thought. A flash of the old Drago, giving extra credence to the new. Fortune was not completely convinced, but then he didn't need to be. All he needed to do was play along with it for a few minutes, just to see where it went. Who could resist?

Fortune said slowly, "You're placing your own trust in the power of God and your own personal charm?"

Drago said, "It worked for Alessandro de Verini."

"I'm not Alessandro."

"I know. But you, too, have had enough."

Fortune sneered again, but he tugged his gaze free of the prince's.

"Very well," he said abruptly. "I'll play. Bring on your Bible."

"Stand up," Drago ordered. "Marco, stand back," he added to the youth. "We need you as a witness to the oath. Esther, the Bible."

While Esther took the big book from his leather satchel, Drago solemnly lined them up on one side of the table. "Matilda, you, too."

Esther laid the book in front of them. Leather bound and impressive, it had "Holy Bible" painted in gold leaf on the front. Their eyes dropped to it, then fastened once more on Drago, wondering what he was up to, what would happen afterward, if there was any possibility that he had *really* turned so far to God that it had made him too trusting.

Esther opened the book.

Drago, holding all eyes, said, "Place your right hands on the book and say, 'On the Holy Bible and before God, I swear faithful allegiance to my liege lord Prince Drago...'"

Three hands touched the book. As they began to murmur the words with varying degrees of embarrassment and barely concealed mockery, Drago's attention shifted, releasing their eyes to glance downward at the book they were swearing on.

It was Matilda who noticed. She broke off her careless oath to blurt, "That's not the Bible!"

At once, Fortune tried to snatch his hand away, but it was too late. As he had once held Esther captive on his bed, Drago held all three hands on the open book as if they were glued there. At the same time, he spoke strange words in an ever-growing voice, filled with authority and so much power it seemed to echo, vibrating through Esther's entire body. She didn't understand the words, but Fortune did.

He began to roar with fury.

Matilda cried, "What's happening? John, stop him! Stop him!" And Fortune abruptly abandoned his anger, instead reciting a counter spell. But it made no more difference. Drago was prepared, and they were helpless. Their shouts, like their bodies, faded, funnelled into streams of energy that poured steadily into the book. Even Drago's voice fell silent in time, and the only sound in the room was the boy Marco's fearful panting.

Slowly, Esther lifted her gaze to Drago's, watched the frightening blaze in his eyes soften and warm. For her. His lips quirked upward.

Esther reached across the table, picked up the book and closed it.

About the Author

To learn more about Marie Treanor please visit www.marietreanor.com. Send an email to Marie at marie@marietreanor.com or join her Yahoo! group to join in the fun with other readers as well as Marie! http://groups.yahoo.com/sexydelights. Subscribe to Marie's Newsletter at:

http://groups.yahoo.com/marietreanornewsletter.

How many times can one man die?

Killing Joe
© 2008 Marie Treanor

To professional assassin Joe, life is cheap, and crash researcher Anna just another hit. Until his own unplanned car crash changes everything.

Dr. Anna Baird, dedicated to the point of obsession, suddenly finds her state-of-the-art crash test dummy haunted by a weird and exciting stranger—who seems doomed to repeatedly experience the fate he'd intended for Anna.

Lost in a reality only he and Anna inhabit, Joe finds himself falling in love with his intended victim, and ultimately fighting to save her life—because whoever hired him still wants her dead.

Available now in ebook from Samhain Publishing.

Enjoy the following excerpt from Killing Joe...

Anna licked the last drop of whisky from her upper lip. Joe's eyes followed the gesture, making her self-conscious.

Hastily, she hid her tongue again. "This is weird. But the whole situation's so weird that I'm going to tell you anyway. Do you know what we do here?"

"Automobile crash research."

"Yep. We do mock-ups of various situations to test car safety and try to improve standards. Well, we had one such mock-up today, using the dummy that has now disappeared. Just before the impact I saw...I thought I saw the dummy's face change. It became—it seemed to become a man's face. Yours."

His eyes searched hers, but not with either surprise or derision. As if the idea had already occurred to him.

Oh Jesus Christ...

How could either of them believe such a thing? There had to be a rational explanation.

He was in an accident—sustained some head injury I'm not qualified to discover. Somehow, he wandered in here unseen and fell asleep...

So where are his clothes?

He took them off somewhere, obviously in a daze. They're probably in a corridor or something...

But his face...I saw his face on the dummy!

"I'm wondering," she said shakily, "if that—seeing your face—was some kind of warning. When did your accident happen?"

He shrugged again. "About nine-thirty, I suppose."

She drew in a breath. "That's when we tested." And the

dummy had gone. Was it lying around the building somewhere with Joe's clothes? Why would he have moved it? It didn't make any sense. None of it made any sense, unless...but that was impossible.

Forcing herself, she met his gaze once more. "Joe, what does this mean?"

He said nothing. So she poured herself some more whisky and drank gratefully. He hadn't touched his. At last he said, "Has anything like this ever happened to you before?"

Anything like what? Like suspecting a man of changing bodies with a crash test dummy? Was she really that insane?

No! So pull yourself together, woman. Think logically.

She shook her head. "No. At least not really..." She slid her eyes away from his penetrating gaze. "When I first worked here and we set up the crashes...I should tell you my family died in a car crash. I saw it happen from a bus stop where they'd just dropped me. Anyway, I used to...imagine...the dummies were family members. But it wasn't really like that today. Then I knew what I was doing—the test just brought back the memory with extra vividness. This today was...it was like it was *really* you. And I've never seen you before in my life, have I?"

"No," he agreed. "No, you haven't." She had no idea what he was thinking, how mad he thought she was, how scared he was by his own situation. Not very, it seemed. She could find no trace now of the despair she had sensed earlier. He seemed almost resigned, though to what, she still had very little clue.

She returned to her own more immediate alarm. "You know my name."

He nodded.

"And you know where I work."

"Yes."

She took a breath. "Were you stalking me, Joe?"

"Yes."

"No you weren't!" she disputed, perversely. "Stalkers like their victims to know about them."

"Perhaps I was waiting for my moment to get you alone, ask you out for dinner, sweep you off your feet..."

"Aye, right," said Anna derisively, resorting to the language of childhood, which at least lightened his hard eyes, brought a faint curve to his lips.

"You find that difficult to believe?"

"Impossible, actually."

"Why? You are a beautiful girl and when I'm not wearing overalls, I'm reasonably presentable."

"You're pretty presentable without them, too," she retorted, then flushed with embarrassment. His dark eyes glinted acknowledgement, but before he could say anything, she rushed into speech herself.

"But you're avoiding the question. How long have you been watching me?"

He shrugged. "A couple of days."

"But why?"

"You don't want to know."

"Oh trust me, I *do*!"

"Then let's say I don't want to tell you."

"Why not?" she flashed back.

He hesitated. "Because it's got nothing to do with this weird situation." His eyes fell. "And because, for once, I nee— like the company."

She stared at him. His vulnerability was suddenly terrifying, because it gave credence to her own impossible suspicion. "You think I'll leave you to your fate if you tell me? Is it really that bad?"

"Yes."

"You're a man of few words, aren't you?"

He didn't say anything at all to that, so with conscious courage she asked, "What exactly do you think your fate is, Joe? The one I would leave you to?"

He looked up at the light bulb, as if deliberately dazzling himself. "Hell." His lips twisted. "Not the fiery hell children are taught about in school—or at least in the schools I went to. My hell is continually reliving—re-dying—in car crashes."

Her throat tightened unbearably. *Oh Jesus, Jesus, we both believe the same thing...* And her own doubts, her own sanity, counted for nothing beside his pain. Instinctively, she leaned over and with a feeling of great daring put both her arms around his broad, strong shoulders.

Damn it, feel sorry for yourself!

His body was unyielding, hard as she'd known it would be, but warm, strangely exciting. She pressed her cheek to his shoulder, knowing somehow that it was sheer surprise that held him so rigid. He wasn't used to being embraced for reasons of comfort.

"You really believe you deserve to suffer such a punishment? Joe, no one is that bad, *no one...*"

He jerked in her hold. "You don't have a clue, do you?" The words burst out of him with violence, frightening her all over again. Panicked, she pulled back, but his arms lifted suddenly, seizing her, holding her hard against his chest, his hand tangling in her hair to keep her still. "You really have no idea what people do to each other, for no reason worth a damn..."

Her heart thundered. Behind the fear came a hot, leaping

surge of desire. She whispered, "What was done to you?"

"Done *to* me? Nothing I haven't given back worse. I'm not the victim here."

His fingers in her hair, fisting, made her every nerve tingle with warning as well as excitement. Twisting her head in his hold, she gazed up into his face, absorbing each tiny line around his dark, almond-shaped eyes, every crease in his forehead, the texture of his lips suddenly so close to hers that her stomach began to burn. His eyes, the cold, opaque eyes that she was sure never let anyone in, were suddenly a maelstrom you could drown in.

She said, "If your—soul—is trapped inside a crash test dummy, then victim's exactly what you are."

"I don't do victim," he said savagely, and kissed her mouth before she could draw breath.

It was rough, bruising, his purpose to shut her up, even punish her for her unacceptable view of him. Knowing it, she slid her hands over his thickly muscled arms to his shoulders and pushed. It was like shoving at a mountain. Truly panicked now, she tried to speak under his mouth, but the movement of her lips only excited him to delve deeper. While his big hand held her head steady, his tongue, strong and insistent, swept around her mouth, pressing behind her teeth as if to pull her closer.

Bombarded, devoured, Anna could do nothing but let him. Yet as soon as she relaxed, sensation flooded her, sweet and raging. Her whole body burned, the fire spreading from her mouth to her groin, devastating her. She was so wet she could feel it on her thighs. And suddenly his motive didn't matter. She'd had sex while less turned on than this.

Faintly, almost shyly at first, she moved her lips under his, dared to touch his tongue with hers, caress it, and then she was kissing him back fully, passionately, and his arms tightened, pressing her breasts to his chest. She clung around his neck, exploring his mouth with the same urgency he did hers, shivering with delight as his hand caressed her back, her waist, the curve of her hip, then slid up her side and over the curve of her breast.

The pleasure of that made her moan into his mouth. His hand moved, softly kneading, until his palm discovered her rigid, pleading nipple pressing through her shirt. And as abruptly as he'd seized her, he released her mouth.

Her glasses had steamed up. Deftly, he removed them, and his eyes, hot and clouded, stared into hers. Slowly, unable to help it, she touched his face with her fingertips, the lean line of his jaw, the hollows of his cheeks, the corners of his lips.

He spoke with fierce triumph. "You want me."

GREAT
CHEAP
FUN

Discover eBooks!

THE FASTEST WAY TO GET THE HOTTEST NAMES

Get your favorite authors on your favorite reader, long before they're out in print! Ebooks from Samhain go wherever you go, and work with whatever you carry—Palm, PDF, Mobi, and more.